CW01084676

All characters in this
intended to represe

First published in Great Britain 2002 by
BLW Publishing
65 Victoria Road
Barnetby-Le-wold, DN38 6HY

Printed by Journal Printing Co
11 Dunlop Way, Queensway Business Park
Scunthorpe DN16 3RN

ISBN 1-904092-00-4

Art Work on Cover Design by Juliet Wright

Patricia Fredericks was born in 1947 in Scunthorpe, NorthLincolnshire: the youngest of three children. After attending the local grammar school, she married at the age of nineteen, starting a family shortly afterwards. This led to a succession of jobs to fit in with raising a family. As the family grew, so did her ambition to write. Somehow she managed to produce several short stories and plays. This chapter of creative writing became the deciding factor to encourage her return to Higher Education. She gained a BA (Hons) degree at Hull, specialising in British and American Literature with socio-history and feminism. After some years of working as an Office Manager in the Fire extinguisher business, redundancy saw her set up her own business as a part-time seamstress. This in turn, left more time for the development of writer to come to the fore. Hot on the heels of this experience came her first novel, Wedding Deception. Readers can now look forward to a full series of novels, featuring the heroine, Marsha Riordan. We know you will enjoy Pristine Murders and also invite you to glimpse the next in the series, Chaste Man. See back page.

Patricia Fredericks

Pristine Murders

ACKNOWLEDGEMENTS

The author and publisher would like to thank the following for permission to reproduce copyright material as follows:

Faber and Faber Ltd for the poem Contusion from Ariel, 1987, by Sylvia Plath.

BLW Publishing

CHAPTER ONE

'Who's been charged with murder? Three murders? Kerri, slow down, what's going on? Mike's father? Where are you? Damn the phone's gone dead.'

'Who was that Marsha?'

Bill had caught the end of this extraordinary short conversation I had just had with my niece. You might think that his mad rush and bustle through the front door, somehow indicated a flight from demons but you would be wrong. It was an appalling night! Rain and high gales had plagued us for two days and nights. The winds had picked up even more today, so much so, that it was difficult to believe that the roof would stay on. Bill stamped his feet on the doormat and shook the rain of his coat.

'Did I hear you say Kerri? She in some kind of trouble again?' Bill queried.

'No, not her Bill. She said something about Mike's dad and three murders. I'm sure she'll ring back in a minute.' I scratched my head and pondered. 'Sounded urgent though. Wonder if I should try 1471 - see if I can track her down? No. I'll give her a few minutes.'

I sighed as I reached for my cigarettes. They'd been sitting in the wall cupboard above the fridge, well hidden behind the biscuit barrel for all of ten days. I savoured the smell of the tobacco before I lit up. I thought I might turn dizzy and put the darned thing out but no such luck. It gave me a good feeling, that first taste. I inhaled more deeply the second time, thinking of Kerri, Mike and Eddie. It was a pleasant coincidence that my niece had been seeing the son of one of our best neighbours, for almost a year now.

There wasn't a more easy-going man around than Eddie Prescotte. Bill broke my thoughts as he came back into the kitchen, having carried out his daily ritual of sorting out our dog. Jenko has huge beanbags to sprawl out on, tucked away in a corner of the lounge. Whenever he hears Bill come in, he begins a succession of leaps at the lounge door to let himself out. If that doesn't work, he takes to scratching at the door in order to pounce upon his master the minute he's released.

'You okay love?' He asked kissing me and stroking my hair.

'Yes I'll be fine Bill but Kerri is such a worry to me sometimes, especially now she's over at our college. I really need her to ring me back, as in "now". I need to know what's going on.' Bill gave me a peck on the cheek and sauntered off into the hallway.

'Bill? I'm...'

My sentence cut short and banished to that mysterious place called Limbo, Bill tossed two polythene Asda bags at me that I was supposed to catch but missed. Luckily I got to them before Jenks. One held two chicken microwave meals, the other a silk, dusky pink, short sleeved sweater.

'M'm lovely Bill. My favourite colour too. Thanks, what are we celebrating?' I asked, holding it up in front of myself and diving in front of the mirror. 'Well? What are we celebrating?'

'Hellfire Marsha, you can't have forgotten. It's our first wedding anniversary. I know it's not until tomorrow.'

'Joke darling! I haven't forgotten. In fact ... no it's a surprise.'

'What did you say was wrong with Kerri?' Bill queried again. Perhaps he hadn't heard me correctly. That's nothing new. I consider it a reasonable day when he hears at least half of what I say. On the other hand, maybe he's been quietly thinking about it.

'Well, she sounded to be in quite a panic about something but I didn't catch much. The line went dead. Only, you know how she talks and gasps at the same time, I'm sure she said something about three murders and Eddie's been taken in for questioning. It all sounded too bizarre! I could have got it all wrong of course.'

Bill picked up the daily newspaper at the same time as I switched on the television for the evening news. The Regional news came on first and promptly alerted me to the problem I couldn't quite catch over the phone.

'Bill, look! It's Kerri and Mike. Oh no! Oh my God! They're getting smothered and mauled by cameramen and journalists. Bill they're outside the Uni.'

'Here give me that thing!' Bill grabbed the remote from me and turned up the volume. Mike was shouting, flaying his arms around. Kerri was pushing and swearing at the cameramen as they zoomed in for close-ups.

'Marsha I'd better make a call fast!'

He called the station and had a squad car go up and rescue the pair.

'Thank God for high-ranking officers, eh, Detective Inspector Lines?' I said, throwing my arms around him in a gesture of thanks. 'What do you suppose is going on over there?'

We heard the screech of brakes and jumped up together. Bill threw the curtain back with such a force, one of the curtains sprang off the rail. Sure enough, blue-flashing lights reflected all over the street. One by one, every curtain in every house within hearing distance twitched their curtains and peeped or pretended they weren't looking at our house. Always the same. I can never understand why two or three police cars at a time have to sail up the street together merely to deliver one or two persons at most. I'd hoped against hope that the neighbours would get used to the fact that Bill was a policeman and learn to take it in their stride, but I suppose you can only ask so much of your neighbours.

Meanwhile I rushed to the door while Bill started to put the curtain and rail back together again. I knew he'd end up with it all wrapped around himself, especially with Jenks all over him thinking it was a game. Jenks would win hands down. He always does! That was my cue to usher Kerri and Mike into the dining room. I closed the door on Bill and Jenks, sparing Bill any more humiliation until I'd attended to and thanked the police. I switched on the coffee percolator in the kitchen and joined the youngsters in the dining room.

I stood back and took note of the pair of them. Kerri looked as though she hadn't put a brush or a comb through her hair in a month. She probably hadn't. It looked matted as though she'd been sleeping rough. She'd probably done that too. When I think of all the money and time my sister spent on that girl. Designer clothes, the latest hair tints, make up and for what? None of those aids to beauty had been applied today. She looked at me head on. I smiled at her and to myself - a child after my own heart. Not a jot of materialism touched this brave young girl. She was honest and thoroughly passionate at whatever it was she was into at any one particular time of day. God only knows what causes and good deeds she would be supporting this week.

'Aunt Marsha, why are you looking at us like that? We've done nothing wrong! Absolutely nothing!' she blurted out to me defiantly. She attempted to rake her fingers through her jet-black hair in a hell-I'm-in-trouble-already mood, only the fingers couldn't cut a path through. Her hair was strong and coarse like mine; thick and glossy, under normal conditions that is. Where mine is dark brown, hers is a definite blue black. She has her mother's dark blue, terribly penetrating eyes, peaches and cream complexion, long legs and slender figure. In fact she is utterly beautiful! Mike too, is exceedingly good looking. There is Chinese blood in this boy. He too has thick, black, sleek hair but accompanied by huge almond shaped dark brown eyes. Kerri and Mike have recently returned from an adventure backpack holiday around Europe for eight weeks, which accounts for Mike's golden tan. Kerri in her youthful wisdom had taken notice of the media with regards to keeping away from the sun. She'd come home with a light honey tan. As for their clothes! Well! Mike didn't look too bad apart from needing a damned good scrub. His faded black Status Quo T-shirt only had three holes in it, probably originally his dad's; whilst his jeans, both slit at the knees, could have done to cycle through the washing machine twice.

Now Kerri wore denim dungarees with one strap slung over her shoulder, which I surmise, relied on gravity to stay put, for lack of sewing a buckle on. They were reasonably clean, passable but about three sizes too big.

Both wore Doc Martens to complete their current uniform and could well have passed for street urchins, but who am I to say? I'd done all that in my college years. After hugging them both, I managed to quieten down their anger and frustration before it boiled over into hysteria. By that time Bill had rectified the curtain problem with the maximum hindrance from Jenko, whom he couldn't bring himself to say a bad word against, and declared the lounge a safe area to sit in. He led the bedraggled pair through with a look of great anxiety on his face. This puzzled me but I did not let it show. I followed them all with a tray full of coffee and biscuits, holding on to them as best I could. Jenko goes crazy for chocolate biscuits!

'Come on then kids, tell Uncle Bill what all that was about.' He pointed to the television, which he'd made a point of switching off the minute they walked into the lounge. Mike slumped into our great old refurbished chair, attempting to bury himself by picking up one of Jenk's beanbags and pulling it onto his knees to nurse. Kerri remained standing but she erupted first.

'Oh Uncle Bill it's hideous, monstrous and so, - so stupid! It's Mike's dad. He's being accused of murder!'

At this, her strong, bolshie self disintegrated. Her bottom lip quivered and tears spilled over down her beautiful face. Course Bill's a sucker for any woman's tears but when it comes to Kerri he's putty. One arm enfolded her; his other hand went to pat her on the head to calm her down, much as he'd do with Jenks.

'Start at the beginning Kerri or would you rather Mike tell me?' Bill said in his soft Uncle Bill voice.

Mike butted in.

10

'That's all there is to it Bill.' His voice warbled nervously. 'We'd finished our afternoon session at the Art Block. Dad had arranged to pick us up. We were going to pick up a takeaway and show him our holiday snaps. The next thing we know, we have no sooner met up with dad in my room, than Police pushed open the door, barged in and took dad away. We raced down the stairs after them. By the time we'd all got to the bottom they'd got cuffs on dad and they wouldn't tell us a damned thing! They advised dad he should have a solicitor as well! We managed a brief word after a two-hour wait at the station and he said all he could tell me was that dad was being questioned about murdering three women. I couldn't think straight - shocked and confused. Still am!'

Mike paused to swallow in an attempt to rid himself of the terrific lump in his throat before he could continue.

'So we caught a bus and made our way back to college. Just about to go through the main entrance, we're besieged by the Press. You know the rest. You probably saw it all on the bloody T.V.'

He finished his woeful tale, breathing a sigh of relief that appeared to completely empty his body of breath. He slumped back into the depths of the armchair again. By now, Bill's demeanour spelled trouble. His deathly pale, anxious face spoke volumes to me.

'What is it Bill?' Now I was anxious.

'Yes, what is it Uncle Bill? Come on. If you know something...?' Kerri asked calmly yet her eyes darted non-stop from Bill to Mike, Bill to Mike.

'It's about the murders in your area isn't it Mike?

11

There's a big possibility that two of the murders were committed in the Hull area.' Bill said in the gentlest tones he could manage.

'Yes, you must know something about it, it's been all over the local and the national papers for weeks,' Mike said, sinking ever further down into the great chair.

'I do Mike. Yes I do. I know all the facts of the case so far. But surely ... not Eddie...I mean your dad, Mike. It's not possible.'

'It's to do with the dating agency I think Bill.' Mike fidgeted with rips in his jeans pulling bits of thread until the frustration of it all saw his fists thumping down on to his knees.

'Can they do this to dad Bill? It's unbelievable! God the way they went for him you'd think he was the Yorkshire Ripper not Eddie Prescotte the gardener! How could they suspect him of anything like that? It's unbelievable! Not possible!'

'I agree with you Mike. I was over at the Incident Room yesterday when they'd begun sifting through any possible candidates. Now I'd like you two to stay here, I mean until this is over. You can't possibly go back to stay over in the college grounds. You can go only to your lectures, seminars, library work etc. You are not to sleep over. All right with you Marsha, old thing?'

'Too right Bill, I insist. Look, you two are well and truly whacked. After you've had this coffee I suggest you take a shower, slot your clothes in the washing machine and relax for an hour or two, on the sofas. I think Bill and I need to take a trip over to the station and find out exactly what's going on. We'll leave Jenko.

Don't and I mean don't, answer the door to anyone. Got that?'

I had no need to ask Bill if it was okay to do this. His brain worked at the same pace as mine. He'd already whipped our jackets out of the hallway.

'See you both later. Remember, don't move.'

By the looks of them sat by the warm fire sipping hot coffee, it would take a bomb to shift them.

Bill and I were both edgy as we climbed into the car. I glanced uneasily at Bill's lined brow as he flicked on the windscreen wipers. We both watched the great drops of rain beating down on the front car window. It was impossible to see much at all. The storm displayed enough of itself on our car to inform us that there would be little or no let up of this weather. That would slow our journey up for starters. We were both careful drivers but tonight of all nights we couldn't afford to put a foot wrong, even though we needed to be at the station as quickly as possible. Idiot drivers were something we daren't contemplate. We never mentioned a thing about traffic or road-ragers. Superstition is a strange old thing. We both believed if you spoke about those things, Sod's Law would make it happen. So I kept quiet throughout and let Bill concentrate on nothing but his driving, and of course whatever else was drumming through his head.

With a clear run, it took only twelve minutes from our house to the station. Everyone we passed from the entrance onwards nodded at Bill and muttered "Sir". We edged and sometimes pushed to where we needed to be. Bill made initial enquiries then further enquiries before he grabbed hold of my jacket sleeve and we trudged up another flight of newly washed stairs.

We learned that Eddie Prescotte was not being charged, merely held for questioning. As luck would have it, we arrived whilst the solicitor on call was still present. Bill motioned to me to wrestle with the coffee machine and wait.

I waited and waited and waited until finally he re-emerged, having negotiated a time for us to go back tomorrow. An easy feat when you throw rank. We all knew the thirty six-hour rule, but we would be back in the morning armed with a good solicitor, hopefully to arrange bail if no charges were being laid. However I needed time with Bill to see how seriously the police were taking this and to determine what evidence if any, they had to even suspect Eddie Prescotte. My man stayed as silent as the grave as we drove for the late night café, which lay on the A164 close to Bentley I didn't like the looks of him. His brows were mighty furrowed, his complexion still pale and for the first time in ages I noticed him gripping the steering wheel. I knew better than to interrupt that kind of concentration. We pulled up outside Alfie's Night Café. A bit rough and ready but Alfie was a pal of ours and all his punters knew us anyway so we weren't going to frighten away the custom. Bill sat while I collected two large expressos and a couple of doughnuts. I felt our bodies needed a shot of sugary carbohydrates.

'Okay Bill let's have it. This is serious isn't it?'

''Bout as serious as it gets Marsha!' I knew this was uncommonly serious by the way he said Marsha, which decoded means I am frightened for this man Marsha.

'Go on then love.'

'You know these horrific murders we've all been talking about?'

'You mean the ones plastered all over the newspaper? You police call them "The Pristine Murders?"'

'Uh huh. Well, did I tell you why we called them that?'

'No but I'm sure now's the time to tell me.'

'Okay. Here we go. Three women have been murdered. All blonde. All heights between four feet ten to five feet two. All slim and attractive.'

'Yes I remember the similarities.' I said, quickly recalling what I'd read.

'You remember how they were all killed? Stabbed to death with a thin stiletto knife, sometimes three times, sometimes five or six. Then the bodies were cleaned thoroughly, even the wounds; the knives cleaned and the women finally left in clean sheets. All killed in their own homes, would you believe?'

I grimaced and shivered as I tried to picture the victims.

'Yes it's pretty horrible Bill I know, but what the devil has any of this to do with Eddie Prescotte? He's such a nice guy.'

'Well, not wishing to reiterate my sweet, so many killers are "nice guys".'

'Agreed. We've been here before Bill, many times. Such an impasse, but you know what I mean. Eddie isn't a killer.'

'I don't believe he is either, but there's more, and you definitely won't like this next bit!' he said, steeling himself with a show of white knuckles. I felt that was an indicator to brace myself too, so I instinctively gripped my coffee mug and the chequered coloured tablecloth.

'The knives were Eddie's, Marsha!'

I slurped my coffee and spluttered until I lost half of it and watched the chequered cloth soak it up like blotting paper. I had been about to shout "WHAT" when my tongue stuck to the roof of my mouth in a burble of coffee. I remained silent and let Bill finish.

'He said he'd had them stolen along with items of clothing but of course it's extremely difficult for us to believe him because he never reported it.'

'Oh God no!' My head flopped down with a thump as I finally managed to knock the rest of the coffee over. Alfie ran over to us in a flap. He removed our mugs, and whipped the tablecloth from under my sprawling arms, swiftly tackling the brown muddy pool about to slither off the table before my very eyes.

'No worries honey! No worries. More coffee coming up. Hey Marsha, lighten up babe.' His hands fell onto my shoulders in a comforting gesture.

'Alfie, what can I say? How can I excuse myself? Bit of bad news that's all. I would love another coffee though.'

'Two shakes hon, two shakes!' Alfie went about his business while I tried to coax my brain to trip into top gear. Now I knew why Bill looked so damnably glum and pale.

'So what do you think Bill, honestly?'

'Honestly Marsha, looking at the worst scenario... I don't know ... it's all.... too pat somehow. Understand me? Too, too pat!'

16

'Oh, I understand all right. But how? How has all this come about? Bill this is torture!'

'Marsha I'll need you on this. No joke. I need some P I stuff. You up for it? Can you tie up what you have at your office? You know, place it neatly in your pending file?' His business voice came across; believing it would be more effective in cajoling me than his ordinary one.

''Course Bill. We have to help Ed, either way.'

'You mean if he's innocent help clear him - and if he's guilty?'

'Get the best barrister we can,' I said, oozing confidence on the outside but my true feelings were smothered in doubt. Bill nursed his mug of coffee. He turned it round slowly a few times, looked up at the notices in the café, and then stretched his legs some more. I didn't like the looks of him one little bit.

'Bill what is it? There's more isn't there?'

I knew that look. He didn't want to tell me but realised he had no choice.

'Do you remember, a while ago, when Kerri and Mike told us that Eddie used a dating agency without much success?'

'Sure do. We all had a titter about that. I'll never know why Ed of all people, resorted to that. He's an extremely attractive man. Wouldn't think he'd have to go to those sort of lengths.'

'That's right Marsha!' The way Bill said this had a ring to it as in "now we're getting somewhere". He began again. 'Well ... all of those women were matched by the agency to Eddie Prescotte.'

17

'What?' I heard what he said but could not take it in. He couldn't bring himself to repeat it; simply nodded and shrugged.

'So what you're saying is that Eddie actually dated them all; now they're all dead!'

'That's about the size of it Marsha.'

'Oh no! Doesn't look good for him at all, does it? Bill, what about Mike? He's in a state already - and Kerri – she thinks so well of Eddie. Where's all this leading?'

CHAPTER TWO

Hetta, my housekeeper popped in to collect the ironing and to replenish my empty larder with her scrumptious home baked cakes and pastries.

'How many times this week are you to eat this rubbish called take-away?' she said flaying her arms and pointing at telltale foil trays in the waste bin, obviously not concealed well enough. I have to presume that Jenks had pushed his big black nose into our waste bin, on a scavenging expedition and it had remained propped open. I knew this spelled big trouble.

'Don't I cook for you?' she asked in a most authoritative and hotly mutinous manner.

'Hetta my sweet,' I tried the emotional tug, 'you must take at least two days off a week. You must not slave over us. You have your own housework to do. You don't need the money. Your house is paid for. Now, you simply must rest occasionally.'

I could not help raising my voice to her as her nostrils were dilating so fast I felt she would have felled any bull in a ring!

'You 'ave gone off Hetta's cooking. Right?' She barked back at me, arms folded and ready for anything.

'Now Hetta, you know that is not true.' I tried my placating voice next. 'Do you want Bill and me to increase in size until we look like giant Teletubbies? I cannot afford to put on any more weight. Look at me! I am struggling now to keep it down. Your food is second to none. We would not wish for anyone else to take care of us. You know that. All I ever ask you to do is to cook us smaller meals my sweet.'

Oh dear that did it! She stormed out of the room, slamming and banging doors on her way out of the house. This disagreement about our food seemed endless. Ever since we had recuperated from one of our escapades, she has spoken relentlessly about "building us up." If she builds us up any more, we simply won't be able to get through doors. At one time, she fed us healthy foods to "mend up our bodies." Now that we are well, she says we should have appetites like horses and continues to feed us like horses. I would have to get back to Bill on this. Still, she did leave us some of her enormous Cornish pasties and a whole host of other goodies made from recipes brought from her homeland of Poland. I had tried compromise to no avail. Eating was important. In fact to Hetta, it was everything. It was her way of saying that she loved us and wanted to take care of us. This meant more work for me at the gym so that I could eat every crumb without holding too many extra pounds.

I pushed Hetta to the back of my mind. I knew I had offended her. I also knew she would sulk for another week, but I had other things to deal with, like keeping my appointment with WPC Helen Wright at the hospital. We had arranged to meet there to interview Sylvia Miller, survivor of a particularly vicious attack. She had suffered two deep cuts to the stomach, one to the arm and a superficial cut to the head; only emergency surgery had saved her life. Now, although under sedation, the doctors had given permission for us to try to speak with her in the hope that she could give us some clues to her attacker.

'I hate hospitals Marsha don't you?' Helen shuddered as she spoke, walking a little in front of me.

I always felt she might be a little intimidated by me because I was married to a Detective Inspector. It put her on her guard all the time. I hoped in time that Bill's colleagues would treat me differently but I don't think it'll ever happen. Nature of the job.

'I've always hated them Helen. The smell of disinfectant; the sight of doctors' white coats; blue operating gowns and the persistent ritual washing of hands, all make me cringe. Not to mention being surrounded by white walls every hour of the day. Maybe this is what heaven's like Helen. All white!'

Helen smiled. A good sign. She didn't do it very often. I tried to keep in step with her as we marched on to the ward and produced our cards. If it were not for the serious nature of the thing, I would have had her laughing. Sylvia Miller had been settled in a side room with a Police Officer on guard outside, also one on the inside. I think the reason for this was that we've all seen too many films of the bad guy disguised as a surgeon coming to finish off his half-wounded victim. We almost entered her room but I stopped Helen for a quick rethink.

'Wouldn't it be safer to ask at the nurses' station, to check if she is able to talk to us? What do you think?'

'You're right Marsha. We'd better check.' We tried to look inconspicuous: most unlikely with Helen in uniform.

'Good morning nurse. Is Sister about or Staff Nurse? We'd like to question Sylvia Miller, if she's well enough.' Helen enquired offering her warrant card. The young nurse walked smartly off to check. While we waited we couldn't help but turn to a disturbance that had attracted out attention;

21

raised voices to the left of us, just at the entrance to the wards.

'Are you sure you've done this kind of work before? This is the fourth time I've told you. You don't put any kind of soap or detergent on the floors at this time of day. The night cleaners do that. Only clear wash. Do you understand? Clear wash.'

'Yes I know that. But isn't this supposed to be a hospital? Aren't the floors and all surfaces supposed to be scrupulously clean at all times? I am experienced you know. I do know what I'm doing,' shouted the fiery red head, ramming the mop head home into the bucket.

'And don't raise your voice! This is an acute medical ward. We have some very sick people here. Now if you'll empty that bucket of soapy water and fill it with clear hot water we might get somewhere.' The cleaner in charge stormed off with the fiery one flicking a V behind her back. I thought I heard a few choice words following after but I wouldn't swear to it. With that, our young nurse returned, informing us that we could have ten minutes with Sylvia Miller. Less if she fell asleep on us.

'That was incredibly unprofessional don't you think Marsha? That woman, having a go at her boss, in front of patients as well. And why didn't she have the hospital colour uniform on I wonder? Must be new. Can't take a simple instruction.' My uniformed friend grumbled.

'Perhaps they're one short Helen. You know the way they have "bank" nurses and "bank" admin, perhaps they have "bank" cleaners to cover absentees.'

'Must be something like that Marsha. Odd though.'

I looked back again and studied the face of this cleaner.

'You really find that odd Helen?'

'Yes I do. Seems to go all against hospital policy somehow. I know how strict they are in all departments. My sister's a staff nurse on Male Medical.'

I'm not sure why but I felt something odd about it too and stored the information, should I need it at a later date. I still ruminated over this as Helen and I quietly moved to Sylvia Miller's bedside and pulled up two old-looking, grey, metal chairs, wondering if the League of Friends would like to fund some new ones. Sylvia's eyes opened. She looked tired and drawn but she had no sign of stab wounds to her face. I smiled down at her as she lifted a hand to greet me. I took it and held it there all the time that we talked.

'Sylvia, I'm Marsha Riordan. This is WPC Wright, Helen to you. We would like to ask if you can remember anything at all that might help us catch your attacker: anything, no matter how trivial. Please stop if it taxes your strength too much.'

'Behind,' she spoke softly but clearly, 'he came at me from behind...low, gruff voice. I don't think he was that much taller than I was,' she sighed, fighting the effects of sedatives.

'So what do you think he was Sylvia, about five seven, five ten?'

'Not sure.' She turned he head slightly to look up at me. 'I remember looking down and seeing brown suede shoes - brown but stained with something or other and ...' she stopped a moment, to think. 'I remember as his arms came forward he had a brown jumper, on darker than the shoes, yes a brown jumper...

stitching was coming away from the sleeve. That's it – no more.'

Weariness etched out lines around her eyes and mouth. It felt cruel, wanting, no needing her to talk but I knew I'd have to press gently.

'What about smells Sylvia, on his clothes? Smoke, tobacco, petrol anything.'

'Yes tobacco smoke; definitely tobacco smoke on the person,' she said, suddenly becoming a tiny bit animated.

'What makes you say "definitely" Sylvia?'

'Because my late husband was a pipe smoker. Smells nice doesn't it? Pipe tobacco?' she ventured a slow half-smile.

I nodded. I liked it too. Bill smoked a pipe as well as cigarettes. It always gave me a comfortable, secure feeling. Sylvia's face became drawn again and the wrinkles around her eyes became much more noticeable.

'Sorry ... can't remember anything else. It's all gone again and...'

'Thank you Sylvia. That's enough for now. Go back to sleep,' I whispered. I turned away. 'Come on Helen, we'll let Staff Nurse know we're leaving and how do you fancy some naughty cakes at my place? I am inundated with them!'

'Oh?'

'Another story. I'll explain on the way home.'

I drove carefully, more carefully than usual. Ever since Bill had told me about the case, I had tried to imagine

Prescotte not as the killer but as a lovely family friend. But ... Eddie Prescotte was a keen gardener who didn't believe in working in good clothes. His gardening garb had gained him the nickname "Gypsy Ed". Much to the amusement of the neighbours he always wore the same clothes; an old pair of green cords, light brown suede shoes and a long baggy brown pullover with stitching coming away from the sleeve. He did say that someone had stolen his clothes! Who would want to steal his clothes? If he was telling the truth and I prayed that he was, could this be a set up? A spurned lover? A jealous guy? Or more simply, was Prescotte a murderer? Helen put on her thoughtful face on the way out.

'Penny for them Helen. Got any clues?'

'Well actually Marsha, I wasn't thinking about the attack at the minute. I was wondering why you told Sylvia Miller your name was Marsha Riordan when you're married to Detective Inspector Lines.'

'Oh! Well you see Helen I never changed my name when we married.'

'Right! Was it because you wanted to carry on with the name your clients know you as at the Bureau?'

'No. That's the name I was born with. That's the name I'll die with!' came the hotly defensive reply.

Helen's face contorted from one puzzled look to a different puzzled look. However it could not detract from the ruddy, healthy looking face. She was a strongly built woman but in proportion, standing six feet. Her size nine shoes sure beat my sevens. Yet, her spectacular feature had to be her glorious natural platinum blonde hair. She wore it, fastened up in a thick French plait making her face look a little too long.

It didn't enhance the rather Roman nose either but I'd seen her at the Police Ball last December with her locks unfurled and her face fully made up. She looked stunning, enticing and mesmerising the males with her huge pale blue eyes. I'd also noticed that when she's in the company of men, she is able somehow, to make her eyes slant downwards in a coy manner making her look helpless, which she certainly is not.

I liked her most of all for her earthiness. We've worked together on several occasions and I hold a healthy respect for her down-to-earth common sense.

Her size makes me wish I had longer legs, a slender body instead of mine, which is commonly described as a voluptuous one. I would have loved smooth hair too, rather than a coarse thick and mostly unruly mop. To go on with the comparison, I once tried coloured contact lenses in the opticians to see what I would look like with blue eyes as an alternative to my obscure brown hazel. I looked like a large Cabbage Patch doll! Moreover, what I wouldn't give for long eyelashes that would curl. Mine resembled a camel's. They were sort of long and straight. But this digression of thought would get me no nearer to the murderer. I dropped Helen off at the station to clock off her shift and asked her to meet me at the small supermarket in Prescotte's locality. I thought I might as well see if I could pick up the local gossip before Helen and I met for coffee and cakes and another exchange of ideas.

'Morning Rose, Mr Harrow. Are you both well?' I chirped.

'Yes thank you,' they said one after the other.

26

'You must know we're on the map now, eh, Miss Riordan. That's what the telly's done for us.'

'Too right Mr Harrow. It's a right old carry on isn't it?'

'I never would have thought it of 'im, meself Miss Riordan,' came the small voice out of the rotund female body.

'Thought what of whom Rose?'

'You know 'im what's done them murders. That Prescotte chap.'

'Oh, been tried and convicted has he?' I snapped. Mr Harrow quickly rescued the situation.

'Get on with your work Rose, go on. Them shelves won't clean th'selves. Don't look like that! They won't ya know.'

He turned back to me with a face that requested sympathy for having to tolerate the gossip of a small-minded woman attached to his workforce.

'Sorry about that Miss Riordan. Friend of yours is he? That Prescotte?'

'Yes as a matter of fact he is Mr Harrow. We'll have to wait and see if he's innocent or guilty won't we? After all there are some damned queer folk walking about these days. Could have been anybody.'

'Too right about queer folk lass. There's one over there for a start. Can't get no queerer than her.'

My eyes followed in the direction of Mr Harrow's finger. A woman wearing sunglasses and a dark blue headscarf stood over pots of yoghurts and cheeses, examining each one scrupulously.

'Now watch what she does Miss.'

I watched. She had in her bag a container of hand wipes. She took two out and carefully wiped her fingers on them after examining about a hundred pots and placing one in her wire basket. She then took two clean tissues from out of her handbag and dried her fingers.

'Good grief Mr Harrow. It must take her all day to do her shopping.'

'You said it Miss Riordan. Takes all sorts.'

'Why does she hide herself away behind dark glasses and dark coloured headscarf?'

'Search me love. Hey and look over to the corner there.'

I again let my eyes follow this instructive finger. A man took half a dozen steps towards the soup counter, turned and walked back, then repeated this exercise another six or seven times. I asked Mr Harrow what this was all about.

'One of them obsessive comp comp ...summat 'o sort people who has to do something so many times before they can get to do another action. If you follow my meaning.'

'Yes, well thank you Mr Harrow. Do you see this sort of thing very often? People who are suffering from, what shall we say, compulsive disorders, disturbing personality traits?'

'No, but there is another one – a man who comes in here quite regularly. Never does no 'arm though. Staff are used to 'im an'all. We tries to 'elp 'em if we can like. It's an illness so I'm told. Can't 'elp it can they poor souls?'

''Course not Mr Harrow. I'm pleased you're such an understanding manager. Even when people are ill, they have to shop somewhere. Keep up the good work.'

I idled my way around the store picking up the same bitter tongue, each aisle that I ventured down.

'Fancy living in the same area as a murderer,' 'don't know what the world's coming to.' 'So close as well, you could get killed in yer bed nowadays.' My trolley more than nicely stocked up was by now actually overflowing. I pushed, shoved and steered my trolley awkwardly towards the checkout. If Hetta sulked for a week, we'd have to feed ourselves. That meant I would be slaving laboriously over the cooker. I had a job to do! Had Hetta no heart? I was an investigator not a cook or a laundry maid, or a baker, or a domestic cleaner. I was more than hopeless at these things. I could sew, oh I was a brilliant seamstress but sewing is not half as exciting as being a P.I. I'd have to think of a way to hold out the olive branch to Hetta.

Loading the groceries into the boot of the car I spotted Helen parking up. I waved and shouted to tell her to press on and meet me back at my place. Our cars followed one another out of the car park. Creeping slowly, as the traffic had built up quite quickly, I spotted the woman from the store, donned in headscarf and dark glasses. She pulled a shopping trolley purposefully and effortlessly, although it looked brim full with sticks of celery and flowers sticking up at the top of it. Her handbag slung over her shoulder she made a good pace to wherever she was going, home most probably, when an unkempt youth came at her from behind grabbed the bag from her shoulder and pushed her headlong. I pulled in quickly as best I could to allow the traffic behind me to pass.

It was then I saw Helen pull up, jump out of her car and sprint after the attacker. I rushed over to the woman stepping over potatoes, onions, carrots and heaven knows what else, that had fallen out of her trolley, but comfort was the last thing she needed. Blazing mad, she struggled to balance herself. About to race off in pursuit herself when I hauled her back.

'Leave it love you'll never catch him. An officer is trying. Here, let me help you.'

'I don't need any help, thank you,' she replied brusquely, 'I'll get him! What I won't do to him when I get hold of him. Castrate him that's what! Men! All the bloody same! You wait! I'll get him.'

'Hey now, come on calm down.' I said, 'Are you hurt anywhere? Look!' I pointed to her scraped knees. They weren't bleeding badly but they looked sore sure enough.

Helen ran back. She'd lost him of course. I say 'of course' because by the time she'd managed to jump out of the car and give chase through the jostling spectators, the thief was streets ahead of her.

'Was there much money in your bag Mrs...?' Helen asked.

'No. Just enough for my shopping. About two pounds in change. I don't use credit cards, only cash. Always careful me.' She gasped and coughed and went on, 'You expect this from men though don't you? Not a woman's trick this.'

'Don't kid yourself. Women can be just as desperate as men can't they Marsha?' Helen chipped in, panting from her chase.

'And how!' I said as quick as a flash. 'What is your name Mrs...?'

'It's Miss if you don't mind. Stop calling me Mrs. It's Miss Diane Somers.'

'Right then Miss Somers. We'll help you with your shopping and give you a lift home.'

'No you won't. Thank you very much. I have no truck with the police either.'

'But Miss Somers you've been attacked. We would really like to help you.'

'A likely story,' she replied curtly and totally unconvinced.

'Miss Somers. Let us take you home or at least to Casualty. We all suffer from shock you know.'

'Will you stop bothering me. I'm all right!' she shouted back.

'Please!' I said as Helen and I tried to look suitably expectant.

At last she agreed reluctantly. I can only assume she thought she would be rid of us much more quickly if we dropped her off home than if we tried to talk her into a short drive to casualty or even a trip to the station to make a statement. As it was, our journey took five minutes in all even with the slow traffic. Helen and I had scooped up all the vegetables from the path and kerbside and shoved them haphazardly into her shopping trolley. Needless to say it would need sorting out. She tried unsuccessfully to talk us out of helping her into the house. Realising she was on a loser here, changed her tune and invited us in for a cup of tea. Talk about changeable people.

A worthy check in my diary later would reveal if a full moon was imminent. Helen hauled the trolley onto the kitchen floor but immediately halted when the wheels of the trolley veered off the kitchen mat. Helen's astute observance spotted thunder on the face glaring at her.

'Not on there!' Somers screeched. 'Don't you dare let the wheels touch the cushion-floor. Leave it there. I'll take the potatoes out from there and put them into the vegetable rack.'

'I wonder, Miss Somers, if perhaps you should bathe your knees first, so that we can see that you're not too badly damaged?' Helen suggested.

She thought about this for a minute or two. 'Yes ... yes I suppose I should do that.'

'Shall I put the kettle on for you?' I said, intending a gesture of kindness but she snapped again.

'No don't touch anything. It's all perfectly clean and germ free!'

'Oh right' says I, feeling humbled and perfectly germ-ridden.

'You two stay here in the kitchen. I'll see to the kettle and tea when I come down. I won't be many minutes.' We both nodded obediently.

'Helen, it must be awful to live like this you know.' I gave my buddy the five second potted history that the store manager had shared with me. I had no chance to hear Helens's comments either way because Miss Somers was back with clean clothes on clean knees, minus her dark shades and headscarf. I held my astonishment as I recognised her at once as the defiant cleaning lady from the hospital, wondering at the same time if she had spotted Helen and myself there.

We had in fact been standing relatively close to her but she had shown no recognition of us. We'd see what came out of our conversation. She brewed the tea, explaining that she always drank the best, nothing but Earl Grey, which neither of us looked forward to. We were not allowed into the lounge although we offered to take off our shoes. We could only peer through the lounge door as the Earl Grey was left to brew. The saying of "a place for everything and everything in its place" sprang to mind at first glance. Nothing had gone undusted, unpolished, or unhoovered. Windows, glass ornaments, glass cabinets, smoked glass coffee table shone like crystal. Three glass ashtrays sparkled like crazy as the sunlight bounced off them. I shouldn't think any of them had ever seen a cigarette.

We were allowed to sit at the kitchen table for our tea. I glanced at the stainless steel sink unit and the taps. Brand new! At least that's what you would have thought. Helen broke my thoughts when she said,

'I really have to say Miss Somers, your home is absolutely ship-shape and Bristol fashion.'

'Yes I make it my business to keep the place clean. You never know who's coming to call. Take yourselves for instance,' she announced proudly.

'Do you entertain visitors very much Miss Somers; family friends?'

'No, no, no certainly not. I'm waiting for Mr Right to come along,' she laughed half-heartedly. I managed to have a good look at her then. Beforehand she seemed to shy away from us but now she'd received a compliment about her home, she looked me full in the face. She was a pretty woman. Eyes almost turquoise blue to contrast her fiery-red, fuzzy hair - good complexion. I'd guess her age at around thirty-five. Her smile was generous and showed off a very even set of creamy white teeth. She looked even younger when she laughed and tossed her head back.

'I thought you didn't like men Miss Somers?' Helen asked, remembering her comments earlier when her bag had been snatched.

'Oh, er yes I was angry then. Who wouldn't be? I've just started a new job. I'm having to fit all my housework in with work outside of my home now.'

'Oh where are you working?' (As if I didn't know).

'I've started as a domestic at the hospital. Started this week, Tuesday.'

'Right. Do you enjoy it?' I feigned enthusiasm.

'I'll get used to it. When I've shown them how to do the job that is.'

'What's wrong then?'

'It's germs!' she rasped indignantly. 'You know how germs spread in a hospital, with them radiators on day and night. Right breeding ground. I'll soon be in charge of cleaning the floors. Then I'll show them how to do it.'

We let her spout off while we drank or rather forced down the Earl Grey and one biscuit each. That's all we were allotted, then checked to see if we could do anything to help her. As her reply was in the negative, our conversation and patience stretched to the limit, we took our leave. Once outside, I asked Helen's view on this meeting with Diane Somers and her obsessive nature of cleanliness. I asked her if she could think of one word to describe the state of the house. She needed no prompting to mouth the word 'pristine.' I promised Helen we'd keep in touch.

CHAPTER THREE

I arrived home well in time to cook Bill a meal. This caused me gross irritation. He would have spaghetti Bolognese because it was the easiest thing to do and I'd bought a bargain of a sauce mix, i.e. buy one, get one free. If the first one refused to abide by my culinary skills then the second one might stand a chance. Besides, tomorrow night we were eating out.

Bill arrived home on time, which happened rarely. I had taste-tested my Bolognese, which was quite magnificent. Again this is a rare occurrence. I had cooked enough for the four of us, laid the table and shouted Kerri and Mike down from their sanctuary. Kerri skipped down on her own, explaining that Mike was fast asleep. Did I have any news?

'No nothing yet, sorry Kerri. Wait until Uncle Bill has taken a shower. He might be able to tell you something. Can you wake Mike up so that we can eat?'

'Oh but we've eaten Aunt Marsha! We had those microwave meals and a load of cakes that Hetta brought. It was all right wasn't it? I mean that wasn't your meal we ate was it?' Her skin bloomed cherry colour and her eyes rolled at me like she'd just busted ghosts in a haunted house.

'Gosh no, stop worrying. Bill usually brings them in, in case we talk until the early hours. If we can't get to sleep he comes down, makes us coffee and puts the snack in the microwave. They usually get stacked in the freezer. We don't like to be without. That's all Kerri. No mystery! No problem. (Can't really tell her we keep them in for when Hetta takes umbrage and refuses to cook now can I?)

'Aunt Marsha? Will it be okay if Mike and I take wine upstairs? We're still in the spare room on the bunk beds by the way. Is that okay too?'

'Well you can take the other bedroom if you like. It's not a double bed, it's a three quarter but you might be more comfortable the pair of you. ... ...Oh for heaven's sakes, don't blush like that Kerri. Feel free. There's a Frascati in the fridge. Help yourself. For goodness sake girl treat this place like home. Oh, that reminds me have you contacted your mum.'

'Yes, done all that.'

She towered over me, her long hair hanging loose, freshly washed and smelling of herbs, threw her arms around me and gave me a hug. She turned to go back and nearly bumped into Bill who in turn hugged her and kissed her to give some reassurance. She then zoomed up the stairs three at a time back to wake Mike, two glasses in one hand, the bottle of wine in the other.

'M'm this smells nice Marsha.' Bill mused taking in the cooking smells. I wish he wouldn't say these things to me. What that really means is: I do wish you'd stop this warfare with our cook and let sanity reign.

'Thank you darling.' I replied in the nicest possible way. 'If you would like to open the Bordeaux sir, dinner will be served.'

'Oh yes. I see. Confidence oozing out of you. What do you know that I don't?' This is Bill's character coming full to the fore. He hates, simply hates it, if he thinks that I've discovered something before he has, particularly if there's a remote chance it may be pertinent to a case he is working on. I spoke winningly to him, stroking his dark brown to salt and-peppery locks, gazed into the pools of his big brown eyes and kissed him. All of this must have had an adverse effect as his face then took on a most fearful anxious expression!

'Sit, sit, sit husband of mine.' I implored, skilfully dishing up his dinner. 'Bill I have a most ridiculous notion!' I started with enormous enthusiasm 'Do you suppose it could have been a woman who did these killings? I mean is it a possibility?'

He thought for a moment.

'Course Marsha, the possibilities are endless. Why? You got a hunch?'

'I may have Bill but give me time to establish a motive or at least a connection in this case. Now is there any line you'd like me to pursue tomorrow?'

'I did hope that you'd come with me tomorrow love. I've permission for us to speak to Ed. Not only that, I think our problems are mounting.'

A frown creased my forehead as I listened to Bill with my ears but trespassed into my own thoughts at the same time. Lordy, lordy! If I could have imagined the wild goose chase this would have led me on I would have kept my big mouth shut. In my quest for reasoning the innocence of Prescotte, I had unwittingly thrown myself a red herring that would prove to be a massive time waster.

'Guess who's leading the case.' He looked down and started playing with his food; half winding his spaghetti onto his fork and letting it drop off again. He never looked up when he said the name Steve Lockburn. The name itself was enough to make me drop my fork.

Unfortunately it didn't drop in a sensible manner like Bill's, it slid right under the pool of sauce.

'Sit still love, I'll get you another one.' He scraped his chair back along the kitchen floor and moved lethargically to the knife drawer while I sat, elbows nestling on the table, with a miserable face cupped in my hands. I knew that if Steve Lockburn handled the case it would be "game, set and match". Ed wouldn't stand a chance. There are good cops, bad cops, antagonistic cops and some bloody-minded ones. The latter is the category I'd put him in.

'Marsha, whatever … if he's innocent or guilty he'll need a damned good solicitor from the word go.'

'I know sweetheart. Well depending on how things go tomorrow I've an inkling, no not an inkling, I know who I'll ring tomorrow. I'm gonna get Maeve Bradshaw in on this.'

Bill groaned.

'God, Marsha can you imagine Lockburn and Bradshaw, swords locked? Still, she is the best. Yes go ahead, give her a ring tomorrow anyway. We'll need a 'canon' to out-shout Lockburn.'

'So be it Bill. Now starving ourselves will not help anyone's cause. Let's eat.'

They said at the station we could go in at ten-thirty with an escort to speak to Ed. It turned out to be a most unsettling drive because it involved utter silence. Bill knew we would get ourselves into a state knowing what we were up against. I suppose you could say we had an emotional personal stake in all this and would have difficulty being objective.

Ed had always seemed to us, to be not only an excellent neighbour but also a good friend too. Yes, I could say in truth that we were more than a little apprehensive. The police car park could not have held another vehicle, not even a bicycle. We managed to squeeze our way into a space that the gods must have allotted us and then I found myself waving at Helen backing her car out pretty sharply to let another car in. She signalled to us again before driving away. It was deep breathing that accompanied us up the stairs, the kind that sounds like a couple of worn out trains. However any arguments with Lockburn had been ruled out. We had agreed not to be at all antagonistic - that is, as long as he didn't wind us up too much. If he became too abrasive I feared that Bill would explode. In some ways Lockburn was a good cop but he had a wicked tendency to draw conclusions from evidence at face value. His logic said "black was black and white was white." Never allowing for grey areas and different perspectives from other quarters, he became renowned as Steve Myopic and not only at this station!

We were close enough now to hear Lockburn's voice booming, becoming angrier and louder with our every step. Bill walked straight through the half open door dragging me behind him. I felt Bill's hand squeeze mine ever so tightly. No this was not endearment but anger. On the way up we could hear the echo of his voice. It had dominated and smothered poor Ed's defensive pleas.

'Oh it's you Inspector Lines, Marsha.' From the way he groaned "Marsha" I knew he was not overjoyed to see me there.

'Inspector Lockburn, do you think we could have fifteen minutes on our own with Mr Prescotte?' Lockburn's jaw dropped two feet.

'I'd rather stay if you don't mind,' he said brusquely! 'See if you can get a bloody confession out of him because I sure as hell can't. Look at his face. Guilty as sin man.'

'Lockburn, if *you* don't mind!' Bill said. It promptly shut him up but he would not sit down, preferring to prowl around the room like a panther.

'Now then Ed, how are they treating you in here?' Bill asked Ed but glared at Lockburn at the same time.

'Not good sir, not good at all. Talk about harassment. I think he invented it.' He glowered at Lockburn, who could not resist jumping in,

'Now you look here sunshine....'

Bill's eyes looked acidly into Lockburn's as he asked him to step outside of the room, pushing me out ahead of them both. He pointed down the stairs and motioned to me, indicating that I should practice a disappearing act and wait in his own office on the floor below. I tried to hasten my retreat but forced myself to linger immediately I was out of sight, making sure I was still within hearing distance. Needless to say I never made it to the office, I remained on the stairs, crouched down listening to every word.

'...Lockburn, he is not your sunshine,' Bill had cut in, 'and if you continue with this I'll refer this case higher up. Understood?' This was Bill's attempt to calm troubled waters.

No that was not understood as Lockburn's tongue flayed viciously.

'Right!' Lockburn screamed at Bill, 'so we're both bloody inspectors – but this is my case not yours! I'll conduct it as I have been trained to do, otherwise....'

'Otherwise what? What will you do Lockburn? I'm surprised you're still in the force, let alone ranking Inspector. Now, continue to harass this person and I'll get you off this case so fast you won't know what's hit you. It's time you kept your temper in check, stopped intimidating people and got down to your job properly.' That silenced him long enough for Bill to speak to Prescotte.

'Ed, I have to ask you some questions. I have to ask you first of all where you were on the dates that the named women were murdered?'

Bill slowly and painstakingly helped him to put the pieces together over the last few months. As it happened Ed kept a diary. He attended so many functions at different gardening societies and attended a group at the library that helped people to track down their ancestors. Obviously it would help to be able to see the diary in order that he could verify if certain events took place and if Bob had actually attended them. Believing his diary to be at his home Bill offered to fetch it only Lockburn revealed why it would be an unnecessary journey.

'We have his diary, Inspector.'

'Well have you had these dates checked?'

'No! What's the point? He did it! There's no one else even in the frame. Christ it's so bloody obvious.'

'Where is the diary please? I'll take it with me and go through it day by day.'

'But you can't. It's evidence.'

'Really? So why aren't you using it then? Fetch it now Inspector Lockburn or do I give the Super a ring? Oh - and in one piece if you don't mind.'

I heard Lockburn blaspheming heavily at the top of the landing and another door slammed. It sounded as though he'd trounced off into another room to cool off. Then Bill took up conversation with Ed. As his voice was lower and calmer, I had to creep back up the stairs a short way to hear what was being said.

'Eddie, old man, it's impossible to have any kind of conversation with you here. Keep your chin up. Marsha and I will come back Tuesday with back up. I mean with one hell of a solicitor. Okay man?'

CHAPTER FOUR

Maeve Bradshaw was her usual brisk "no nonsense" self when she breezed into my office on Tuesday morning. It was not difficult to find. Bill had bought me this cute little building precisely because of the convenience of its locality - in Cottingham Road, close to the railway station. I'd asked her to be prompt as we had a great deal of work to do.

'So you think he didn't do it Marsha? What makes you so sure? He's a man isn't he?' She scathed with a twinkle in her eye followed by a mannish guffaw hard on the trail of her twinkle.

'Maeve, if I said he isn't the type, you'd immediately get up from your chair and go home. No, it's all too pat. Like an elaborate set-up. You know, you've seen plenty. So your next question is, "has he got an alibi?". No, I'm afraid he hasn't. We've been through his diaries with a fine toothcomb. Oh, all his appointments are valid and he kept them, every one. Unfortunately ...'

' ...at the time of the murders he was sitting by his cosy fire, sucking at his cosy pipe, watching his cosy television,' she cut in abrasively. 'When can I see him Marsha?' She then enquired in a more business-like manner. 'I've set it up for eleven o'clock this morning. They won't let me in of course but you'll have no problems. Will you take it on Maeve?'

'I'll tell you that when I've spoken to him.'

I gave Maeve the documents to pile through and went to my small kitchen to prepare more caffeine and also to reflect. Nothing had changed with her.

Still the thick brown elastic band held back the coarse grey hair. It must have been three years since I'd seen her. She'd been forty-nine then and looked not a day over sixty! I wished she'd get rid of those hideous rounded spectacles that do no justice to her face. Mind you even a little blusher or eye make-up would help alleviate the yellowish tinge to her skin and hide the black rings around her eyes. That's because she reads non-stop. I turned and glanced. She looked up and glanced back at me smiling. Lor ... I hated it when she smiled. She has crooked teeth top and bottom that don't appear to sit properly together whether her mouth is open or closed. Her smile always reminds me of an angry German Shepherd dog. Her shoulders are broad like a man's and her hips, which are even broader, are usually clad in tweed. The first time I met her she resembled a huge woolly pyramid. Bill joked when I tried to describe her to him. I remember him saying, he supposed she wore twin sets, pearls and brogues. Well he supposed right! She does!

One of her amazing gifts is that she can skim read faster than my laser printer can print off. By the time I'd assembled coffee, biscuits and teacakes she'd gone over the papers and joined me halfway between the kitchen and my desk, declaring facetiously,

'I find all of this so very odd my dear!'

'Oh? Have I missed something then?' I always feel obliged to ask such silly questions when in the presence of brilliance.

'Marsha, the stiletto knives are the defendant's. Right?'

'Right.' I replied.

'The gardening clothes identified by the surviving victim are of course the defendant's too. Right? Then why in God's name aren't we looking for a psychopath my friend? A murderer does not leave clues hanging about. Nor does he wear the same clothes he gardens in to perpetrate murder. He would destroy them. He simply wouldn't keep a collection of knives, using them one at a time to kill people with and then wait for the police to come and find the remainder in his knife draw or wherever else he might keep them. Tell me Marsha, is he what normal females call good-looking? Is he all there...? The defendant...? Or does he have a screw loose?'

'Well no! He always seemed quite sane.' I paused a second or two. 'I would describe him as having film star looks though, as would most women. He's well educated and well spoken. Why?'

'Marsha, you young thing, you know this could be about a woman scorned.'

'You don't say Maeve', I replied mischievously. I had to say that because my line of enquiry was exactly so. However she was such a sweetie and had a far larger brain box than myself, I thought I'd let her keep the upper hand and see what ideas she could come up with.

'Okay, Maeve. It all sounds so simple. But how do I prove that the defendant didn't do it?'

'No, Marsha, the thing to do is find and prove who did do it. With my help of course.'

She smiled showing me all her crooked teeth again. I was pleased she was on my side. Anyone else would take that smile for a snarl. I explained briefly that I had discovered a character with a personality disorder who would perhaps be capable of committing acts of violence but nothing substantial that could connect her with the murder. That is, not yet. I was thinking of Somers of course. Yes, she was a strange personality but that did not mean I could accuse her of murder, although I still could not erase the word "pristine" from my mind. The murders, Somers "pristine" house, her talk at the hospital. Maeve and I put our heads together to determine our next move. She suggested that I go and see the Manager of the small supermarket and have another chat with him. In the meantime, I should speak to Bill and have this woman tailed at all times.

'Oh, by the way Marsha,' Maeve leaned sideways and peered over her specs, 'do you still have that enormous great chocolate beast with the intelligence of Einstein?'

'Certainly do Maeve. Why?'

'Because I feel you're going to need him.'

CHAPTER FIVE

I had a lazy evening for once, having cancelled our celebratory dinner and rearranged it for Saturday night. Bill granted my request for a tail on Diane Somers. Now I could concentrate on my problem with Hetta and generally putting the world to rights, sprawled out in my bath tub, up to my armpits in lavender bubbles. God love her! I seriously cannot function to the best of my ability without Hetta's organisational skills working industriously throughout our home. I can't fault her. Our clothes are laundered to such a high degree that persons of blue blood could not complain. As for her cooking, well – all I can say is there has to be a way to show her that she is invaluable to me and greatly loved by us all. Trouble is – how can I explain diligently and tactfully that it is only Bill and I that live here and not the armed forces. I can't waste too much energy worrying about this problem though. For heaven sakes, poor old Eddie is in deep trouble. He's our friend and Mike's dad. I think I really should call back and have another chat with old Mr Harrow. See if he can shed any more light on this Somers woman.

'Mr Harrow, just five minutes, I promise, no more.'

'All right if you're sure that's all it'll take. I've a new promotion to get on the shelves this morning. Can I interest you at all? It's a new butter, low fat and all that. Do you take care of your figure Miss Riordan? Doesn't look like it to me!'

'Beg your pardon Mr Harrow.' Did he have to be damned brazen?

'Ha! Sorry, I didn't mean it in the way you think. I meant yours is as perfect as I ever did see. Real woman you are love. Not like these bean pole girls you see in 'ere.'

'Well, thank you for that.' I shot him a false grin. 'Now, Mr Harrow. It's about that strange woman, Diane Somers ....'

'...Gawd, strange?' He cut in, 'I don't 'alf get 'em round 'ere love.'

'Yes but what exactly do you know about her, apart from her obvious strangeness I mean?'

'Well it's funny,' he cogitated and ruminated scratching his head and running his thumb over his chin, 'but you know that last victim ...somebody ...er...Miller?'

'Sylvia Miller? Yes, what about her?'

'Well, it's only a few weeks ago, that loopy Diane Somers used to watch her go out of the store. She used to wait until the Miller woman got to the door, then she'd rush to pay for 'er own things, then scuttle off after 'er.'

'Oh? Did she rush off to talk to her? I mean did they know one another?'

'No I don't think so. Twice I've been out and watched. When that Sylvia Miller stopped to go to the butchers or the Post Office next door, that Somers woman would stop and watch 'er and wait for 'er to carry on up the street.'

'Didn't you think it odd Mr Harrow? I mean did you never ask her sort of casually why she followed Mrs Miller?'

'Would you Miss Riordan?'

49

I scrunched up my face, 'take your point Mr Harrow. Did you notice her doing it to anyone else?'

'Can't say as I did. I only took an interest 'cos she did it more than once.'

'Thanks very much for your time. I said I'd only keep you five minutes and I reckon my time's up.'

'Right you are Miss Riordan. Shall I save you some bread in the morning?'

'Oh yes please. Thanks for reminding me. See you soon.'

'Pleasure love. See you tomorrow.'

I had a gut instinct that made my stomach turn over. More and more I remembered Diane Somers strange behaviour. Of course, this could all be coincidence. Stranger things have happened at sea. But we weren't at sea. Eddie's whole livelihood was at stake. I was as convinced that he didn't do it as that madcap Steve Lockburn was convinced that he did. A conviction of ideas was not enough. Every religion that I knew was as strong in its conviction, that, only they held the truth. Wars are started on conviction! Such is conviction! No, I knew better. Empirical evidence is what courts demanded. I toyed with the idea of ringing Maeve for a working lunch at the local at the end of our street, the Golden Calf. I had time to kill. Then I thought again and decided I might go and visit Sylvia Miller again instead. She may be feeling a little better today.

Sylvia was sitting up in bed chatting to a nurse and enjoying a cup of tea. It was ten-thirty. After a quick check with the Staff Nurse I meandered over to Sylvia.

'Hello there. Remember me? Marsha Riordan again. I must say your looking better already. How do you feel?'

'Hello. Yes I vaguely remember you. Came with a young policewoman didn't you? To answer your question, I'm well ready for home but they say not for at least another week,' she said despondently.

'After what you've been through Sylvia, I rather think that's wise don't you? I'm sure they know what they're doing.'

'You're right of course, I just feel like I've outstayed my welcome. Have you come to ask me some more questions?'

'Only if you feel up to it.' I said pleasantly with my fingers crossed behind my back.

''Course! Nothing else to do in here is there?'

'Sylvia, I wonder if you know of or are aware of a lady in these parts called Diane Somers.'

'You mean that woman who dresses up in dark glasses to go to the supermarket?'

'You know her then?'

'No I don't know her Miss Riordan - caught her following me sometimes, you know. Never knew why. Just took it for granted we had a really sad person in the neighbourhood.

'Did she ever threaten you at all? Or did you ever find her intimidating?'

'No not really,' Sylvia looked thoughtful. 'But why would I? There's one in every neighbourhood isn't there.'

Disinterested she changed topics. 'Anyway what's going on with that lovely man they've got for murder. Now don't look like that, I do read the papers! I don't believe it's him at all. I was all set for a date with him, I was.'

'Really?' My ears pricked up like a giant elf's.

'Yes. Look if I tell you something, would you promise not to tell?'

'Yes,... as long as it's not police business.'

'No, no. It's just that – well. I joined one of those dating agencies. Fed up with no male company around. He's the one I'd have loved to have gone out with.'

'But I thought you never met the person until the date. I suppose that's rather naive of me. Got a photograph of him did you?'

'Sure. It was all proper like. Handsome devil he is. He's no murderer Miss...er...'

'Riordan, – Marsha.' I prompted quietly.

'Hasn't got the eyes for it.'

What a sweetie, I thought. Unfortunately that wouldn't hold any water in a court of law.

'There isn't a woman round here hasn't noticed him about. Mark my words.'

Sylvia started to rub her eyes. I could see she was tired and wincing a little.

'Thank you so much for your help love. Is it all right if I visit again?'

''Course it is. Glad of the company.'

CHAPTER SIX

I needed some good old fresh air and exercise. Walking Jenks always encouraged me to thinks things over; clarify my thoughts. Bill would be late home tonight so Jenks and I would pick up a take-away. I had to ask myself, how and why Somers was a prime suspect in my mind. What did she really have to do with anything? Was she a murderer? She could be. But then so could Eddie Prescotte. I suppose I had not for one minute considered his guilt, only his innocence. As far as I was concerned Diane Somers nestled nicely in my mind as prime suspect but how in the world could I prove it? This case was as weird as any could be.

The evidence at present of course pointed to Prescotte; the clothes, the knives and he'd also dated each of the dead women. To add to that, it now seemed as though Sylvia Miller had experienced a near miss with her date. Unfortunately that too was Eddie Prescotte. Everything pointed to him but it was impossible. He can't have done it – can he? What possible motive would he have for killing these women; all blonde and petite? Diane Somers framed a medium height neat figure, clear skin but red hair. I wondered if she'd stalked Bob for some reason...

Lost in my thoughts I didn't hear Helen's car drive up until she was nearly on top of me. Jenks wagged, barked and bounded up to Helen as if she was his long lost friend.

'Any luck Helen? I'm exhausted trying to pull inspiration out of my brain. You find anything?'

'You'll never believe it Marsha but Lockburn's crossed swords with your old man again.'

'Oh? Now what?'

'Inspector Lines said to tell you that Lockburn's been taken off the case. You won't like this next bit. Prescotte took a real beating in the cells last night.'

'Oh God not that!' I sighed. 'Did Lockburn instigate it?'

'I dunno Marsha.' Helen stared down at her horrid black shoes, her shoulders slumped, her hands stuffed loosely into her pockets, 'You know how ranks close in and register complete denial...'

'Say no more Helen. How bad a shape is Eddie in?'

'He's in hospital with a broken jaw at least and both his eyes are black.'

I pulled the mobile phone from my handbag and rang Bill who confirmed everything Helen had told me.

'Come on Helen, hospital.'

Bill sat in stunned silence at Eddie's bedside. He'd been taken to a side room for maximum protection. Or so I was told. Eddie had endured the beating and no one had asked for a doctor until Bill arrived this morning. Needless to say, Maeve would have a field day demanding a full investigation and wouldn't stop until she'd got it.

I approached Ed's bedside but Bill held his hand up towards me.

'He's dozed off sweetheart.' He said miserably 'Come on you two, we'll have coffee in the canteen.

We never spoke a word as we made our way through the corridors, following the signs to our destination.

I could see that Bill was more than upset. His quietness and the look in his eye told me he was livid. Helen detected this too, so she diplomatically grabbed a tray and joined the queue. Bill and I spotted a table in the far corner of the giant clinically painted room and robotically pulled up our chairs.

'I don't understand what the hell is going on here Marsha!' my poor husband blurted out. 'Is Jenks with you?'

'Yes, he's in the car probably sound asleep. You look beat Bill. Is this why you're working late?'

He nodded glumly. 'Wasn't going to tell you at first. God knows what we're going to tell Kerri and Mike.'

'Why did Lockburn go so far? None of this makes sense.' I chuntered.

'Well apparently, when Lockburn was hauled in and duly suspended, he said he only meant to get a confession out of him and frighten him. Yet, this new bloody P.C. Macmillan, that undisciplined idiot with the ginger hair, he really flayed him. It's appalling, bloody appalling.'

'Red hair huh?' I asked quietly, mulling things over.

'Yeah. Red hair.' Bill sat quietly now. Helen trundled back with the coffee and scones. There we all sat for a full ten minutes looking so miserable you'd think we'd all been made bankrupt. Helen made an effort to draw us into conversation again.

'Where do we go from here guv?'

'Not sure for the moment Helen. Eddie's taken a nasty beating. I can't help wondering that something more than a confession was required here. Like someone had a hot desire to kill him.'

Helen and I both shivered.

'Have you checked up on Macmillan, Bill. I mean, he's pretty new to the force. Has somebody missed something vital here if he can blow up so easily? Was there more than one policeman involved - in the beating I mean?' trying to sound animated instead of lethargic.

'No only him, on Lockburn's instructions of course. God, the papers will have a field day.'

'Funny, that's what I said to myself about Maeve's reaction when she starts.'

Bill laughed ever so slightly.

Bill', I said with trepidation, 'what would you say if I told you I thought I knew who had done these killings but I don't know how to prove it?'

'I'd say, with your brain girl, follow your hunches! Laborious detective work Marsha. That's what'll find the answer. Sheer doggedness.'

We drank our coffee, which I can only describe as putrid. We also nibbled our dried-up scones without enthusiasm and in mutual silence. Afterwards Helen and I left Bill outside the canteen. I'd asked Helen to accompany me to Sylvia's ward. This was not to actually speak to Sylvia again, more to ascertain Somers's movements or rather her working hours at the hospital. If I could learn exactly when she was at work, then I would know when her house was empty. I also had reason to be well pleased with myself for donning soft leather, flat shoes. We certainly covered some mileage marching around the maze of corridors.

Back at the Female Medical ward I nudged Helen to

56

do the talking. She described Somers but gave no name. Yes! They had a new starter of two weeks that fitted our description, a Miss Diane Roache. We thanked her and gathered details of her working times. Armed with this new information we finally arrived back at my place via the take-away.

Jenks was full of it. He appeared to look upon Helen as his new permanent playmate. I took her hysterical laughter as politeness. After all, who likes a ten-ton chocolate monster piling into their body and washing them all over with a great long coarse tongue. I banished him to his basket in the kitchen. That was one problem out of the way but sure enough within seconds another promptly shot up out of nowhere.

Mike and Kerri, both ran straight at me, tearful and nervous. I apologised for having no more news and asked them both to be patient. I was sure we'd have him home and dry in no time. I packed them both back upstairs. Helen read my thoughts.

'What on earth will you say to them next Marsha? There's every chance this will go straight to the Crown Prosecution Service. The evidence points so strongly to Eddie.

'I know it does but we've a great deal to cover before that happens. I'm sure Bill will stall as much as he can.'

We walked into the lounge having slipped our shoes off. Lo and behold there sat Hetta, hugging herself in Bill's armchair. She too was distressed.

'Oh Hetta, please don't. Not you too. Come here.' Today of all days I needed this like I needed a hole in the head.

Shyly, she then moved towards me and without warning practically hurled herself at me, clamping her arms around me in a crushing bear hug that would squeeze the life out of a tree. I couldn't decide for a second or two whose affection I dreaded the most, hers or Jenko's.

'I am so sorry Marsha. I have behaved very badly. I am a simple countrywoman who has been selfish. I...'

'...Enough Hetta! That's quite enough. You know too well how much we love you. We want you to be happy, that's all. You do so much for us, we're intent on you staying with us forever.' I continued this diatribe patting her on the back as Helen watched wide-eyed. Lord only knows what she made of our family dynamics. I soothed Hetta in approximately six minutes, praising her for her wonderful selfless care that she lavishes on Bill, Jenks and myself. It worked. She promised to be back tomorrow cooking our usual meals but in smaller portions as long as she was allowed to bake an apple pie with the best apples in England! Naturally, I knew full well that the pie would be large enough for Desperate Dan but what could I say?

I now had my housekeeper back, which was one thing less to worry about. Soon the whole house would be sparkling and shining, back to its immaculately tidy self. Meals would be on time, clothes ironed and one hundred and fifty thousand toilet rolls would be stashed high in the loo. I bid her goodnight and sat down to talk with Helen.

We knew that Somers would be on duty from seven until eleven in the morning, disinfecting the whole ward if she had her way. I didn't fancy asking Bill for a warrant yet.

I was in fact, almost sure I would find nothing incriminating at all in her house. Scrupulously clean and tidy would be a gross understatement. I would not have thought that her state of mind would allow for anything tainted to touch her super-clean home. However I may glean something more of her character.

Helen and I agreed to drift round in the morning at eight-thirty and I would break in. I couldn't risk taking Jenks on this excursion as dog hairs, particularly chocolate coloured would be left on her cream rug. She would know someone had been in. I was also amazed that Helen never batted an eyelid. She agreed, reluctantly, that if anything went wrong and we were sussed, then she would have to arrest me rather than put her own job in jeopardy. With a plan in my head, I bid Helen goodnight. I opted for a brisk shower followed by a small glass of whisky. I relaxed and settled down with my novel while I waited for Bill to come home.

Hetta, having resumed her duties at breakfast time, put Bill in a good coping-with-the-day mood. I did not relate my plans for the day to Bill. In this instance, I reserved the right to the privacy of my profession. If I found anything at all, I would refer back to him. Course if he knew I was up for unlawfully breaking into someone's home, he would lock me up! I threw my arms around his neck giving him his morning hug and kisses being watchful not to overdo it. Sure as "eggs is eggs" he would have realised instinctively that I was up to no good.

Helen arrived dead on time. I had to be nice to Jenks because he hates staying behind. Still, secretly,

Hetta adored him and spoilt him rotten. I had pre-arranged with Helen that we would both climb into our respective cars and drive to the vicinity of Somers' house leaving our cars in a nearby cul-de-sac. Helen's car could not help being a huge give-away. On official duty driving a panda car, she was taking a huge risk on this escapade with me.

Now I am not proud of the fact that I have an incredible photographic memory of locks but then again, I make no apology for it. Dad had said that every good P.I. should have this knowledge, for the right reasons obviously. Those being that, if ever you were locked in by the "baddies" you could escape! So when Helen asked how we were going to break into Somers' house without breaking doors or locks I cast her a shadowy look. She couldn't bear to broach the subject again. Our shiny cars stood side by side in Mapletree cul-de-sac.

Two streets away we somehow had to gain entry to Somers' house without disturbing the neighbours. Easy! We opted for a swift fence hopping and leaping over back gardens trusting to the gods that snoopy neighbours were still in dreamland or at work. Luck on our side, we managed it without a hitch. Systematically we worked deftly. Both of us experienced in what we were doing, I took upstairs, Helen downstairs. I would like to say that we did it all in a record twelve minutes and our mission was fruitless.

I checked every nook and cranny, searching for anything that might give us a clue that she lived some kind of double life. Every room the same: pristine! I would imagine that even homes of Royalty may accumulate dust here and there but in this house, there was none. In fact, the mystery of it quite absorbed me.

I wondered if Hetta might know the secret. Windows and mirrors showed no trace of fingerprints dust or blemish. Dressing tables with ornaments displayed complete symmetrical positions, as one would expect from a person having obsessional traits. In the bathroom not only were the towels beautifully soft and clean, oh no, they hung at exact levels even to the matching stripe of each towel. There were pots containing soap but alas, even the soap looked as though it had been washed and dried before being placed back in again. Cleanliness to an absurd extreme did not denote a home but a showcase. It also made me sad for Somers. Helen experienced the same downstairs. The oven she noted, after putting her head in it, was so shiny you could eat off it. We'd been meticulous in that whatever we had moved, took care to replace things exactly where we found them.

After examining and cross-examining our movements, before we moved off, we could not resist peering into the shed. It looked odd! I suppose odd might not be the correct word. Empty – that was the word. The shed was not only empty but also pristine clean. Not a thing in sight! no lawn mower, no spade, no gardening fork, not a trace of anything. The floor and walls were bare. Helen squashed her nose trying to get a better look. She could see that the floor looked damp as though it had recently been washed. This took our interest. Could we somehow gain entry without attracting anyone's attention?

'Morning! Can I help you?' Shouted one of the nosy neighbours.

'No thank you sir, we're fine.' Helen shouted back.

'What is it you're looking for?' The question directed again at Helen.

'Police business sir, thank you.' Helen replied with a gritting-your-teeth smile.

'Oh I dunno, I think we citizens have a right to know what's going on when the police come snooping around our gardens, don't you?' he persisted.

'It really isn't your business sir but if you must know, someone in this vicinity has a sick dog that's run off and is about to give birth. She may be hiding in a shed or outhouse.'

'Oh right. Shall I keep a look out then?' queried our good citizen.

'Yes sir, that's kind of you but don't lose any sleep over it. It can't get far, the state it's in. I hope the dogcatcher finds it before long. We were in the area so we trying to help out.'

'Right then. Bye constable.'

'Goodbye sir and thanks again.'

I shrugged my shoulders smiling to myself. 'Who taught you to lie so well Helen? Haven't heard that one before.'

She winked as if to say, "It's not important is it?"

We called at Alfie's for coffee. After mooching over me with one hundred requests of how he wished me to eat and drink, he left us alone.

'What do you make of that shed Marsha?' Helen asked, trying to sip a huge cappuccino coffee without the froth clinging to her nose.'

I thought hard whilst I tried to stir the grated chocolate into my own coffee. 'Now, you know on the one hand, everything is exactly as we would expect to find it – right? On the other hand Helen, why would you completely empty your garden shed of all its tools and scrub the place clean unless you had lots of naughty things to hide. I mean where are the garden tools? And apart from the obvious obsessional motive to clean, why scrub the floor of the shed and remove every trace of anything that's ever been done there including cleaning dead bodies!'

'Marsha get real! If Somers is the murderer, you can't tell me that she kills her victims, hauls them over to her shed, scrubs them clean, then takes them back to their houses; possibly also the scene of the crime and then wraps them in one of their own sheets waiting for them to be discovered.'

'May I tell you my friend, that sometimes, fact is stranger than fiction. How do we know what goes on in the mind of a dysfunctional or disturbed personality? How do we know this isn't exactly what took place? How do we know that she hasn't the strength of ten men?'

Helen laughed heartily after seeing the twinkle in my eye.

CHAPTER SEVEN

We had managed, at long last, to be sitting in our favourite restaurant enjoying our celebratory anniversary meal. Jenko had a special doggie meal prepared for him and against all the rules of hygiene sat with us under our corner table, the one specially reserved for our visits. God alone knows what Environmental Health would have to say. We'd done this before on many occasions. Only one person had complained to date but Luigi's staff cleverly hid our chocolate monster until the Health Inspector had done his thing. Being regular visitors here, our friends know Jenks and how extremely disciplined he is. Not only that, he plays to an audience, any audience. We enjoyed our steaks in red wine and I could have eaten a thousand of the profiteroles covered in hot chocolate sauce.

About to make a start on our second bottle of Sauvignon and another profiterole, our blissful evening was declared null and void by the various gods of war.

'Just what the hell do you think you were doing snooping around my garden madam? Did you have a warrant to come onto my property...?' screamed one angry Diane Somers.

I opened my mouth to deny I had ever been near the place when she fired again on all cylinders, finishing off with,

'...What a load of bull! Looking for a lost pregnant dog, my eye!'

My eyes, although wide open, were full of innocence when I turned them on Bill. He responded by lifting one eyebrow like Mr Spoc, the logical, knowledgeable Vulcan from the Enterprise.

'Miss Somers do you mind! I'm trying to celebrate my wedding anniversary with my husband...'

'I could get you into an awful lot of trouble lady. I know who he is,' she raved pointing a finger at Bill. I thought he would have to resort to escorting her out of the restaurant but Jenks saved us the trouble. He had crept from under the table with enormous stealth, stood behind her and let out a sharp gruff growl, kind of like a young grizzly bear. She jumped back, nearly knocking a chair over and off she went again with her raving.

'What's this gross animal doing in here? I'll have the law on you. Not above it you know, the likes of you two! Can't do what you like you know. People like you have got to be stopped.' Jenks stood tall now, baring his incredibly white teeth. That evoked the correct response. She backed away, grabbed a chair and held it against herself as if Jenks was a lion about to pounce and she the lion tamer. I winked at Jenks who knew exactly what to do. He scedaddled under the table, through into the restaurant kitchen door and was immediately ushered to our waiting taxi, Alfie.

Like a true soldier he whistled Jenks into the car and threw a blanket over him. Although our mad woman ran after him and screamed demands at the management to call in the Public health people, the rest of the diners roared with laughter. On the downside, I had to declare my clandestine visit to my spouse, whom I hoped had mellowed with the wine. He would not report me this time he purred pleasantly. Seeing I was a winner here, I tried to give him a potted history of her comings and goings until finally I blurted out that I believed she could be a suspect for the Pristine Murders.

I did not realise that the more red wine I drank, the louder my voice became. My sweet Bill put his fingers to his lips in the hope that I would quieten down.

'Shush – sweetheart,' he murmured. 'We'll discuss it in the morning.'

I didn't want to think at all about the morning. Here I was having a wonderful romantic celebratory dinner with my man. However, he did have something interesting to disclose. He was relaxed and thoughtful.

'My sweet, angelic, beautiful wife I have something to tell you. I know I said we wouldn't talk shop tonight but there is an important development I was saving for you. That Macmillan chap, you know, the P.C. who blew a fuse and beat up poor old Eddie, well you'll never believe this, but he was actually bailed earlier this evening.'

'Oh? Who'd be so stupid? Can they do that? I mean it's a serious offence for a policeman Bill?'

'I know, but Lockburn stipulated quite clearly that Macmillan was under orders. The authorities have let him out on bail under the supervision of one of his cousins. A cousin by the name of Cameron Somers.'

'What!' I sprang upright in my seat. 'You do realise who that woman was don't you Bill. Diane Somers.'

'Indeed, my lovely wife. I know all right! What's more, I don't want you anywhere near her or her premises again unless I'm with you. Understand?'

I love Bill when he's so masterful... or shall I say assertive in a masculine way.

Sylvia Miller gained strength and eventually left the hospital with the duly appointed Social Services help. A strong-minded woman, she did not intend to let this incident diminish her own hold on life. Helen and I visited her at home in the hopes that she might remember even a tiny detail that she could not recall previously.

'I'll make the teas shall I Sylvia?' Helen volunteered politely, as was her way.

'That'll be lovely dear, thank you. Biscuits in the left hand cupboard above the work bench.'

'Let me shake those cushions up for you love; make you more comfortable and let's have your feet up.' I purred in mumsy fashion.

'You are a pair of old fusspots. Don't think I don't know what you two are up to, 'cause I do,' she said, aiming a knowing expression my way.

'Oh?' I said innocently.

'Yes. You want to know if I've remembered anything else don't you?' I held my breath whilst nodding a "yes", a little lost for words.

'Well, I do. And what's more I think it's a woman'

I heard a gasp and rattle of cups from the kitchen. My eavesdropping colleague had picked up every word. This was not too difficult as Sylvia had one of those rich clear deep voices. Helen made a clumsy entrance with the tea tray not wanting to miss a single syllable.

'Kettle won't be a jiffy Sylvia. I'll make myself at home shall I?' Helen shone delightfully.

'Come on then Sylvia. What makes you think it's a woman?' I asked, hoping against hope that my suspicions might be correct after all. She rested her head back on the newly plumped up cushions and stroked her forehead with her fingers.

'Do you remember I told you that I could smell pipe tobacco on those clothes?'

Helen and I both nodded together not wishing to interrupt her train of thought or suggest things to her that might embroider her memories and tell us what we wanted to hear.

'I can say for certain that I remember the smell of a woman's perfume. I tell you how I remember it, 'cause I buy it myself. It's one of those Avon ones, Soft Musk. Really strong too. And I'll tell you something else. The arm that went round my neck had a bracelet on it. I could see a couple of small charms sticking out of the sleeve of the old jumper, then a piece of chain. Not a thick one like a man would wear. No, it was a small linked one. Funny the things you notice when you think you're about to die isn't it Miss Riordan?'

'Yes it is Sylvia, only it's Marsha - call me Marsha and this is Helen. Now, I'm going to ask you to do something for us that you may not want to do because it will be emotionally painful and perhaps frightening for you....'

'...I know what you're going to ask me Marsha,' she cut in confidently. 'Will I go through it step by step so that you can take notes? Yes I will because I'm ready. Need to clear my head of it now.'

'You really are a brick Sylvia. Would you mind at all if we used a tape recorder? That way we won't have to

68

keep stopping you while we write it up. Have you given a full statement to the police yet?'

'No, I haven't. Said I hadn't to until I felt well enough.'

'Okay, I'll tell you what. When you've told us as much as you can, we'll have it typed up. You can check it over in your own time and sign it and we can use it as your statement. How's that sound?'

'Just the job girls.'

'Now take your time and think carefully.' Helen said, switching on the tape recorder.

'Well – I'd gone outside to see if Tibby was anywhere to be seen. I'd put her food out by the shed door. That's a little way down the garden path. It wasn't dark, more dusky I'd call it but I had the light from the kitchen and the outside automatic spotlight giving me all the light that I needed in that area. I was late giving her supper 'cos I'd dozed off. Had some lovely music on the radio that afternoon. It lulled me off to sleep you see. Silly really. I'm only forty three.

'Anyway I put the dish down, was about to stand upright when I felt this hand around my throat. I was terrified I can tell you, scared to death but I'm stronger than I look. I reached up to grab the arm, trying to pull it from my neck when I felt this sharp pain to my stomach here on the left side. I let go of the arm to feel my side when I felt a sharp stab to my right. I lifted my hand up. It was crimson red. By now I became more angry than scared so I started to grapple with the knife. That's when I got it in the arm as well. But I did manage to turn around. The man/woman had one of those balaclava things on. Looked horrible it did but instead of trying to pull it off, I pushed it upward to try and take it off, that way.

I saw some hair sticking out; queer hair, black curly, fuzzy, you know like a doll's wig. I remembered that well, I did. How strange it was.'

'The other thing I noticed was the colour of the eyes. You notice things like that don't you, I mean if they're not a straight forward blue or brown, more like a greeny blue, turquoise blue. I could have been wrong of course, because artificial light isn't quite the same as natural light is it? Funny colour for a man, though, I thought at the time unless he was a foreigner. Anyway, I could smell the perfume. Can't mistake that for a minute. Been buying it for years. And the charms on the bracelet I mentioned. Two of them peeping out from the sleeve.' We must have looked blank as she added quickly. 'You know a baggy sleeve that had been turned up a couple of times. I got a good look at one of the charms though. I'd swear it was a little silver teddy bear. Couldn't quite make the other one out though.

Anyhow... then... I felt another blow around my head. I remember screaming one hell of a scream. Seemed to have found my voice at that stage. That's when he or she bolted. I collapsed on the steps of the back door. Mrs Allerton heard me. Came racing across and dialled 999. She was ever so good. Came with me to the hospital and stayed 'til they got me sorted. That's it girls - exactly how it happened.'

'You've been absolutely marvellous Sylvia.' I congratulated her. 'Now I have to ask you if you have any idea why anyone, man or woman, would have reason to attack you at all?'

'None whatsoever. Get on with everyone I do; haven't an enemy in the world.'

'What about that woman who used to follow you from the supermarket Sylvia?'

'Wouldn't know her from Adam love. She always hides under them silly headscarves and glasses, does that one. Real strange.'

I thanked her immensely as Helen and I took our leave. We promised to look in on her later in the week, strictly on a social visit. I had then rung Maeve to give her a quick update on what Sylvia had remembered and arranged to meet up at the nearest pub for lunch and discussions.

It was two minutes to one. Maeve was already at the bar ordering her lunch. She waved us over to join her. This was handy and convenient! I shouldn't have been so surprised. It was after all one of Maeve's favourite haunts. She lunched here regularly and so knew the best time to eat. She then walked over to the table she had claimed for the hour and motioned to us to join her there.

I could not help but stare after her and wonder how any woman could have been blessed with such a manly face. I moaned about mine lots but Bill liked it. Said he'd never seen such amazing eyes, that couldn't decide whether they were green going brown or brown turning green. Despite my feeble dieting and exercise regime, Bill never stopped loving me or giving me compliments. A prince among men, he rarely mentions my shortcomings, my faults and especially my daily moans about my spreading figure. I pride myself on being a modest person. I would never want people to even consider that I might be spiteful or conceited or any of those things!

It is good to be completely honest! – Isn't it? So - if I was a man and about to try and make Maeve a compliment on her looks, I wouldn't know even how to invent one. This is a shocking thing to say about someone but unfortunately it's true! But then I did say I have my faults. Yet - she was stalwart as a friend! I would never let negative thoughts about her image throw me.

Apart from Sylvia's story, I had come up with nothing particularly fruitful that morning. My aim was to search over and over again, to see if I had missed something in the file, something that might instigate Somer's arrest. Maeve could have found something.

'And how's my fearless friend today?' she seemed to snarl lion-like.

'Hi Maeve. Sorry, I'm not in good fettle. I'm at a full stop. Can't find a thing that would link the attacks with the Somers woman.'

'That's because she hasn't done the murders girl, that's why.'

I jerked the sandwich away from my mouth, 'Oh Maeve', I spat out with tragedy written all over my face, 'but I thought you...'

'Yes, yes, yes,' she growled again impatiently, 'but we all change our minds, don't we girl? It was a thought to pursue at the time. One to be pondered and discussed – accepted or rejected - pure logic. We then examine a possible outcome, change our minds again – sometimes a hundred times over, well, don't we dear?' she pressed home. 'Close your mouth Marsha!' she continued with her griping, 'you're looking so gormless and stupid!'

'Yes I imagine I do! Go on then,' I prompted.

'Right. Now here's how I see it. I had a good think about what you said – I'm talking about your interview with Sylvia, right? You are presuming that because of the bracelet, smell of perfume and black curly wig that the murderer is a woman dressed in a man's clothes. Prescotte's to be precise. Couldn't it just as easily be a man in a man's clothes wearing a woman's perfume, woman's bracelet and woman's wig in order to have precisely the effect it has now manifested.'

I pushed my half-pint glass around on my beer mat and studied Maeve for a moment.

'Now why didn't I think of that?' I chastised myself. (Knowing full well that I had willed myself to believe that Somers was the killer.)

'Because I'm paid to think Marsha.'

'Aren't I Maeve?' I said feeling more than a little put out.

'Never mind that. We are at present presuming the accused is innocent.'

'Go on.'

'You realise that I have to consider the vehemence of Lockburn. If he hadn't stopped the beating when he did, Prescotte would in all probability be dead by now. Of course we both understand that the police will do their damnedest to arrest any offender as soon as is humanly possible. Their superiors and the public for that matter, demand it from them. So you have Lockburn wanting an immediate result and,' Maeve fuddled with her spectacles for a moment, 'Prescotte could be as guilty as sin. What's more, Lockburn could even know or suspect with good reason – reasons we are not aware of – that Prescotte is guilty.

73

It sounds to me like he was driving mighty hard for a confession.'

I waved my hands around and shook my head adamantly.

'No way is that man guilty Maeve. That is one of life's impossibilities. On top of that I firmly believe that Somers is involved here somewhere. She's not given her correct name for a job at the hospital for a start. Then P C Macmillan happens to have a cousin, one Cameron Somers who bailed him out. No come on. She has to tie in somewhere.'

'Now look, Marsha my dear,' Maeve spoke all mumsy to me, you know one of those "heart to heart" jobs, 'just because Diane Somers follows people around, it doesn't mean that she's a murderer. It could be sheer coincidence that she shadowed Sylvia Miller. It could also be a coincidence that she is related to Macmillan. Let's face it from what we've learned she follows anybody. Yes, she's a sick woman but that does not make her a killer.'

'Point taken Maeve but where do we go from here?'

'Well after lunch I suggest that we pick up Jenks and go for a short ride out of town, to the home of Cameron Somers. Let's at least see if we can either gain some positive information or once and for all eliminate Diane Somers from our enquiries.'

'Now you're talking.'

CHAPTER EIGHT

We drove straight to the market town of Beverley, with surprisingly little traffic to hinder us. There we were to interview Cameron Somers, hopefully to find another lead. We had no trouble at all finding his home, a large bungalow immediately North West of the town centre, towards Molescroft. We had to force open a wooden latch gate to reach the garden path. An overgrowth of ten years would not adequately describe the state of his garden. If you ever wondered who had the most dandelions in England then Cameron's garden had them, standing a startling two feet high.

The outside of the building and the grounds gave the impression that it was not inhabited. The ragged curtains were closed and the windows would have adored a good old soak let alone a wash. We knocked anyway.

Sure enough, Cameron Somers answered our persistent knocking. On the surface he appeared amiable as he ushered us into the dark dusty lounge, where he promptly introduced us to his cousin P.C. Macmillan. Oddly enough it seemed that they were pleased to see us, which knocked us back somewhat; even though it may be difficult to imagine them having callers at all in that den of iniquity. We managed to move enough beer bottles and mouldy bread papers, off the chairs, in order to sit down. We also declined their generous offer of coffee or a can of beer without offending them. Satisfied that we had avoided some kind of bacteria entering our bodies, Maeve opened the conversation.

'Thank you very much for seeing us Mr Somers. I am the solicitor acting for Mr Anthony Edward Prescotte. This is Miss Riordan, Private Investigator.

We are trying to gather information that may help us to establish Prescotte's innocence and enable us to track down a murderer. Will you answer questions on this subject?'

'Fire away,' Somers answered with an attentive look on his face.

'Now first of all, could you tell me please where you were on May 29 of this year sir?'

'Ow the 'ell should I know? Tell me, what day was that?'

'It was a Monday sir, a Bank Holiday in fact, if that would help your memory.'

'Not 'alf lady. Me and Mac here, we went to the races. Do it every Bank Holiday.'

'Do you have any proof of that Mr Somers?'

'I'll say. We put a bet on every time we go. Still got the betting slips from the meeting. We save them. Sort of keepsakes. 'Ere look! This is our scrapbook! Me and Mac, we've been into horses for some time.' Macmillan stayed quiet but Somers walked over to his old, chipped sideboard cluttered up sky high with rubbish. Sure enough there was the evidence; betting slips stapled together. There were hundreds of them, together with train tickets, photographs of horses and any manner of memorabilia shoved into shoeboxes. Then Macmillan threw in his valuable snippet of information.

'We've been doing this since we were kids. Our Diane comes with us sometimes. Not often though, you know with her being so clean and tidy an' all. She 'as to save up to stay in a hotel. Won't stay with us.' He laughed, 'says she'd like to disinfect the place very time she comes near us.'

'Oh!' says Maeve and I together.

'I don't suppose she came with you on the last trip did she?' I asked, trying not to sound too curious.

'Matter of fact she did. Stayed at one of them posh hotels in the town centre.' Maeve scribbled furiously, taking down the name of the hotel so that we could run a check ourselves.

'Do you find your cousin's habits of cleanliness obsessive Mr Somers?' Oh dear, both men laughed uproariously.

'Too right. Not too sharp in the head is she Mac?' Cameron looked to his cousin for back up.

'Ain't that the truth. Even stranger 'cos her mother were never like that. All our mothers were sisters, see. Only none of 'em were like her. No idea where she got her stupid 'abits from,' he'd continued. I tried another tack.

'Well it sounds as though she certainly rubs along okay with you two but when we've spoken to her, she strikes us as not liking men. Would you agree with that?'

'Oh yeah! That what she says. Believe me if she could find a good-looking bloke wi' plenty of cash she'd grab 'im wi' both 'ands. But I ask ya. You really think she'll keep a man – never! Too damned faddy 'bout the 'ouse. Screw loose that one. Follows people around for no reason.'

'Would you consider her dangerous to anyone though?' I persisted wondering where all this could possibly lead us.

'Good Gawd, no!' they sang out loudly.

'So why do you suppose she would change her surname when she applied for a job at the hospital?'

'Well wouldn't you if you had a stack of psychiatric reports behind you, especially for a job in a hospital. Come on now. Take a great leap with your imagination.' It was Macmillan who braved the obvious.

'What name did she use then?'

'Roache. The name mean anything to either of you?'

'Ha! That's easy! It's another family name. People do it all the time.' We seemed to have exhausted that road of enquiry so Maeve asked him delicately why he'd found it necessary to beat Prescotte to a pulp. She had to watch her wording as he was suspended from duty. We didn't want him going for harassment charges too but were startled by his reply.

'Only too pleased to help out there. Maybe I shouldn't but sometimes the temptation is too great. I'd have done it if Lockburn had told me to or not.'

'So it really was Lockburn who ordered you to beat him up?' Maeve asked keeping her tone level and low. Macmillan became agitated. His brow sweated, dripping into his full ginger bush eyebrows. His eyes narrowed.

'All right! So I wasn't supposed to kill him. "Get a confession out of the bastard" that's what he said, only ... I went berserk didn't I?' His face bloomed and his fists clenched, showing off his strong white knuckles 'Killed one of my mates' sisters didn't he? That one they found six months ago. I remember it well. Another bloody Bank Holiday. Some real screwball you got there.

Always does 'em in on a Bank Holiday. Did ya know that? No, by the looks on your faces I don't suppose you did.'

'But what if the police discover the real killer and you had beaten Prescotte to death? You'd have been standing on a murder charge yourself. Don't you see that?' I said becoming more exasperated by the minute.

'Look!' he growled venomously, 'if there's one thing I can't stand, or rather two things, it's women killers and child killers. Justice is only seen to be done rarely. This is a lousy job I do! What happens to crims, murderers, and rapists? Few years banged up and they're out again, walking our streets. There is no working judicial system anymore. It's archaic.'

'Hey calm down Mr Macmillan. We think the same way. It takes years to change laws. I am in full agreement with you. So is most of England. The majority of us believe the punishment never seems to fit the crime. I would like to see a fairer system. More police around for starters, to clean up the streets. We all want the same. But if you take the law into your own hands then the law will jump on you. We can't change the law that way. Who was this girl that you know: the murdered girl?'

He paced, breathing heavily, trying to find his words.

'Bradley Bates, my mate, it was his kid sister, Ruth. Twenty-five; a sweet, real cute little blonde. You women would probably describe her as petite. What chance did she have trying to fight off a maniac? Eh? What chance? I know it's that Prescotte. I know inside. It's a gut feeling that we've got the right man. I'm absolutely sure of it.' His fist banged down hard on to the small table, shaking an ancient aspidistra plant that looked parched enough to drink a river. The bitter silence that followed, killed any sign of more conversation. I nodded to myself and said quietly,

'I think that'll do for now and thank you very much for your help, both of you.' We left both men ruminating in their respective armchairs.

Back in the car, Maeve and I decided that both men were telling the truth. We called at the hotel that they had told us about and questioned the staff, checked records and sure enough, Diane Somers had been there the day of the murder. No doubt had we checked all the betting slips we would have found some of hers too.

'Marsha can we call at the station before we turn back to your place for tea?'

'Mm surely.' I said, wrapped up in my own thoughts and contradictions. 'What for? Something else on your mind?

'To check on the dates of the other murders.'

'Think there's some significance here then?'

'Well, New Year's Day is a Bank Holiday, May 29th also a Bank Holiday. If the other murders are recorded as occurring on a Bank Holiday it may lead us to think of other possibilities. For instance, every full-time working person has the Bank Holidays off. Most people at any rate. Let's check first.'

'Yes but the trouble is Maeve, it could be an unemployed person doing it on Bank Holiday's for that very reason, to throw off suspicion.'

Sergeant Trout knew Maeve as soon as she walked in. In fact I smiled to myself, fully aware that Trout and most of the station were afraid of Maeve. I was sure she'd procure any morsel of information she asked for. As it happened, the murders were committed as follows, Jan 3 Bank Holiday Monday, April 24 Easter Monday, May 1 Bank Holiday Monday and the attack on Sylvia Miller, May 29, Bank Holiday Monday. Today was August 18 The next Bank Holiday fell on August 28. Maeve and I stared at each other, stupefied.

I could relate to both Cameron Somers and Macmillan. We had to believe their stories. We could verify every detail as being correct. We even checked out the bookies where they picked up their winnings. As they were regulars, they were well remembered, even down to the pretty cousin with the red hair and the flashing blue-green eyes. Now that was another thing. Sylvia Miller made a big thing of the eyes. This didn't exactly mean anything until Maeve made an acute observation.

'How many different colours of contact lenses can you buy these days Marsha?'

'Oh say no more Maeve. I read you.'

So there we were at the station, gawping at one another realising we'd arrived nowhere trying to find our killer and poor old Ed would cop the lot. However we did hear a whisper or rather Maeve did, that it would be increasingly difficult to even try at this stage to mount a case against Eddie. Maeve was already in the throes of starting a case for compensation for the beating he had taken in the cells. Whether innocent or guilty he has the rights of the "innocent" before being proven guilty.

Up until now, he had not had that right and protection. We also learnt of his release from the hospital, some two hours ago.

My head a complete shed, I asked Maeve to drive us back to my place. Hetta flew into overdrive the minute she spotted Maeve. Here was another body to which food could be stuffed inside! This was always her way of gaining their approval of her I suppose. Hetta, as I expected, practically threw a host of creamed scones, homemade shortbread and chunks of fruit flan at my guest. It had a strange effect on Maeve, who it appeared became so enthralled by Hetta's culinary skills, she invited herself to dinner.

'You may as well stay the night Maeve. If you'd like that is. I'm sure Bill would appreciate some input and fresh ideas from you. In fact, any help at all if you don't mind?'

'Marsha, I'd be thrilled.'

'That's settled then.' I turned to Hetta,

'The menu is of your own choosing tonight. What do you think to that?'

'It is a good day! That's what I think to that!'

Her smile reaching her ears and beyond, she did us proud. After dishing it out so lovingly, we thanked her profusely and insisted she took the rest of the evening off. Over a sumptuous dinner of homemade steak and potato pie, fresh fruit salad, cheese and biscuits washed down with a good Valpolicelli, we three comrades settled into animated conversation. We needed a new lead, as we'd come to a full stop. Bill and I enjoyed Maeve's company so much we invited her to stay on for a few days. I could tell she was flattered, by her ghastly grin. Mutual pleasantries dealt with, Maeve steered us back to the problem in hand.

'You see Marsha, don't you, that although in law I am advising you that we find the murderer in order that we eliminate Prescotte; in truth we have not proved yet that he did not actually do the killings.'

I smiled,

'I know exactly what you're saying Maeve but I am so confident Ed didn't do it that I would bet you a few thousand on it. However, realising you are not a betting woman... oh damn there's the phone. Bill would you be a honey...'

Bill jumped up, excusing himself, to take the call and left us to it.

The call took a good ten minutes, which is unusual at mealtimes. We normally take names and numbers, promising to return all calls after our meal or simply leave it to the answer phone. Mealtimes are so important to us as we plan all our domestic trips such as holidays, days out, decorating etc at meal times.

It would have been naive and futile to ask Bill if something was wrong. He'd stepped back into the dining room like the walking dead. All colour drained from his cheeks as he reached for and sat precariously on a narrow stool. He held fast to the doorjamb to retain some balance, looking from Maeve to me and said,

'Lockburn is dead.'

CHAPTER NINE

Maeve's eyes looked shrewdly ahead, in line with my top kitchen window. Mine looked directly at her. Then I snapped out of the trance and dashed over to Bill, shouting at Maeve to fetch the brandy, which she managed at top speed. He drank the fiery liquid in one gulp, then managed to bring himself back to the dining table, signalling for us to do the same.

'They found him two hours ago. Stabbed five times, body immaculately cleaned, wrapped in a single white sheet!' The silence that crept upon us threatened total despondency.

'Maeve say something.' I pleaded.

'Marsha, Bill, I'm going to make us a large pot of good strong coffee. Marsha take Bill into the lounge, there's a good girl. I'll bring a tray through.'

As the colour gradually flowed into Bill's cheeks, he regained his equilibrium.

'Marsha this is terrible. It's out of hand. Why Lockburn?' I'm away to his house now! It's eight twenty. You two coming?' Bill asked although he already knew the answer.

''Course love. I'll take our jackets. Can you clear it with the station Bill?'

'Already have. Bradley's there... Scene Of Crime Officer. You remember him Marsha?'

'Yes, yes I do. I've seen him about three times, I think.'

'Come on Bill, Marsha, let's crack on. I'll drive. Bill's still a little green around the gills.' Maeve took temporary control to give us a breather.

The house was cordoned off when we arrived, as you'd expect. We nodded to the P C's at the front door and entered without a problem. Bradley saw us from the hallway and waved us through.

'Nasty business Bill. This makes four of these so-called "Pristine Murders" that we know of. Exactly the same as the others only he's not blonde and petite.'

'Oh please Bradley, spare me the grislies. What can you tell me?' Bill snapped, apparently back on form.

'There was a tip off. Not a nice one though. The station took the call. It was one of those jokers who masks his voice with some instrument or other. It said, "Lockburn's dead now. Got a bit too clever didn't he?" Then he rang off. That's all I can tell you Bill. I'm moving the body out now, so you can turn the place over.'

Bradley turned away and continued to scribble in his notebook. We all glanced down at the body. It was unbelievable. Lockburn had been well and truly scrubbed, even shaved. His hair clean and combed was astonishing in itself until Bradley pointed out to Bill in between writing, that the victim's finger nails had been cleaned too. We were all well and truly baffled. What kind of a mind would perpetrate killings in this manner? What kind of a person were we looking for, man or woman? Lockburn was slightly taller than I was, around five feet eight inches, weighing approximately fourteen stone. We were looking for someone incredibly fit.

Bill instructed Maeve over to Lockburn's desk, sent me to begin upstairs and put a call through to Helen to bring her over and give us a hand.

It wasn't long before I spotted Helen from the landing. Bill shouted instructions at her as she made a beeline for the stairs

'I've just started in the large bedroom.' I hollered down to her. 'Come on up.' Fleet of foot, she stood before me in seconds. Now this room looked as though it had never been slept in, it was so tidy. No dirty clothes littered the floor as I imagined would occur in a bachelor pad. Everything looked to be ship-shape and Bristol fashion. We pottered around for five minutes or so, going through his wardrobe and dresser. Nothing appeared to be out of the ordinary. Helen moved on into the spare room and left me to it.

As the minutes ticked away, I noticed that I made much more noise than Helen did, opening and shutting drawers, doors and cabinets. In fact Helen made no noise at all, so I stopped what I was doing and wandered into the spare room to see what she was up to. Spread out on an old fashioned gate-legged table was a huge wad of paper cuttings.

'I was about to call you in Marsha. Come and have a look at these!'

We stood rock still, mesmerised, staring down at the old newspaper cuttings; all separate stories of the murders, spread out neatly but joined together with sellotape.

'Do you think Lockburn was on to something Marsha?' Helen asked nervously.

'Oh God! It's looking that way. Let's delve a little more in this room, shall we?'

I took two steps to the left of me. His spare room or

rather his box room would only allow for this. But other newspaper cuttings were piled up in the corner under the window. They were damp but intact. It seemed that perhaps he only used this room for storage and nothing else. I picked up the yellowed bundle and spaced it out on the ottoman for easy reading. Nothing registered at first until I noticed the story about a murdered prostitute. I carefully worked my way through the pile. All in all there were various articles on prostitutes who had been beaten, murdered or stalked. Helen knelt beside me as I began to read one out:

'The police are trying to piece together a profile of a possible serial killer. All the intended victims were petite blondes'... The papers were two years old. A nasty shudder of apprehensiveness gripped and unnerved me.

'Helen! Listen to where they all lived! The murdered women came from Liverpool, Birmingham; one beaten up in Leeds and the ones that were stalked – Driffield! Oh hell! That is close to home. Lockburn was definitely on to something after all. What do you think?'

Before she had the chance to answer, Bill came up to see how we were doing. We led him into the spare room and watched as he followed our actions rifling through all the old newspapers. Then he grunted and pulled a piece of paper out of his pocket to show us. It had been found on Lockburn's body,

"You're getting too close Lockburn."

Don't look so worried you two, it's not the original. A constable copied it down for me.

'I suppose that's some help Bill.' I said to my better half fidgeting with my hair and pulling my ear lobe, not really having a clue as to why I thought it might be. It simply seemed an appropriate thing to say to my disheartened husband.

'Marsha, Helen, go down stairs and turn his desk out thoroughly. I'll ask one of the men to parcel this lot up and cart it down to the station. The office staff can read them up; see if we can find any clues.'

Helen and I took off our jackets and made a start on Lockburn's desk after we had assaulted the waste paper basket of course. We worked our way through the drawers reading every single thing including grocery lists, receipts for dry-cleaning, anything! Now it was the turn of the bottom drawer to be ransacked but it was locked fast. No keys were in sight so Helen ran back up the stairs to ask Bill if we could force it open. Curiosity brought him back down again as he promptly stomped off to fetch a crowbar from the boot of his car, wasting not a second in doing so. The drawer was a deep one that held a dozen or more files, clearly labelled, the first file "shouting" LIVERPOOL. It contained very little and by the looks of all our faces, our excitement had been cut short and transformed into deflation. There was a photograph of a beautiful young oriental-looking woman. The effort of trying to make out what colour hair she might have, from an old black and white newspaper cutting, had us all squinting but the hair had a definite style to it. It was cut in to a perfect short pageboy style, emphasising her elfin shaped face. Apparently, her identity had never been released to the press. She had simply been transposed into print as a prostitute. I wondered whose idea that might have been. Lockburn's?

Surely not! How much had he discovered? Was he working closely with the Liverpool Police?

I excused myself. I needed some air and a cigarette. Praising myself on the one hand for having little need of the "weed", yet I was convinced it would help me to think. No doubt the medics would tell me it would not help in the slightest but when did my bolshie self ever listen to them? (one of my major faults!) The idea of Mike's mother being dead filled me with horror. That Lucy may be a prostitute, somehow seemed devastating. How in God's name would her son react?

By bringing Mike to the forefront of my mind, my conscience was pricked violently. I'd left him and Kerri to their own devices. I also didn't realise that Bill was on his way into the front garden until I heard the click of the door behind him. Lost in my thoughts, stamping my cigarette out on the garden path he came to put his arm around me.

'Nasty business this is turning out to be, eh, love?'

'It's dreadful Bill – what about Mike?' I asked as if he might come up with a magical solution.

'Don't know Marsha. I honestly don't know. Can't tell him anything yet though. Have to resolve the thing. Do you want to go back home? I'll be a couple of hours yet.'

'Yes I do Bill. I feel guilty at the moment. Not sure why. I can't change anything but I feel I should go back home though, you know, have a coffee with him and Kerri – something!'

'Go on love. Go back and put your feet up for a while. Try and relax.'

We kissed and I walked sluggishly to my car, resolved to walk through my own front door with at least a smile on my face and a look of everyday normality.

After only five minutes with the youngsters, it was apparent that Kerri had tried hard to keep Mike's spirit's up to no avail. He wasn't having any of it. According to Kerri he'd begun to sit by himself for much longer periods, in the spare room that I'd allotted the pair of them.

'Marsha! This whole affair is hideous! My dad has been released without charge but still his neighbours won't speak to him. He might as well be in prison! He tells me to keep away from him until they've caught the killer, otherwise people might start having a go at me. I should be with him. He's no one else. I'm all he's got! Come on! What the hell am I supposed to do? The police are still watching him all the time.' Mike blurted out.

My heartstrings pulled violently! I felt so sorry for this young man trying to make good his life but things were not going well at all.

'I take it you've heard nothing at all from your mum Mike?' I tried but failed miserably to be nonchalant in my manner.

'Oh God! It's months since I heard anything. She just cut herself off. Just like that!'

'Well, think for a moment. How many months?'

'God knows! It must be nearly ten at least. Can't be exact. I'm so busy at college, one day merges into the next: the same as the weeks, then the months. You know how it is. What can be wrong? I know she loves me. We were really close, despite her leaving dad. I know I wasn't around for a while but I never actually knew that they didn't get on, mum and dad. In fact I knew "sod all" about their relationship to be honest. Children never do, do they?'

'No I think that may be true of loads of families Mike. You're not on your own there.'

'Can't think what's wrong Marsha...' He lapsed into his deeper memories,'...and she loved hearing me play the guitar when no-one else did.'

'Mike,' I said confidently, 'you really have to try not to worry. No news is good news. Right? As soon as we've solved this case, I'll get on to it. Bet you I can find her. How long is it since your mum and dad divorced did you say?'

'I didn't Marsha. They never did. Just separated four years ago. She went to Liverpool to her sister's. That's where I wrote to her anyway. Me and dad as you know, well, we've been in Hull ever since.'

I left the questions alone and prepared a tray of food. Mike and Kerri immediately disappeared back upstairs into their private haven.

Liverpool, I mused to myself. Why do I keep thinking Liverpool? The thought then dissolved into thin air almost as fast as it had manifested itself.

An early night had to be on the cards. I needed to put space between myself and the turmoil whizzing around my own head. Bill didn't arrive home a couple of hours later as he thought he would. He never actually surfaced from work until a little after twelve thirty, only mildly disturbing my slumber.

In the morning I woke at seven thirty five. Bill had already risen and gone into work early. I made my way down and promptly started the kettle off for a cafetiere of coffee. Maeve followed directly.

'Marsha I do realise we've only just woken up but I pondered and ruminated for some time last night before finally dropping off.'

I unscrewed my bleary eyes and tried to focus on what Maeve was dribbling on about at this hour and had to force myself to look up at her. She looked grotesque, in fact quite scary! Her hair resembled a giant brillo pad, stuck up rigidly all to one side. Her eyeballs were circled with great blue/green dark rings around them. This image provoked a childhood memory: a sort of witch from Macbeth. The old robe I'd lent her with its ragged sleeves served to emphasise the look! She frightened me! I'm sure she would have frightened Mike and Kerri had they glimpsed her in this state. Thank God they were tired and could sleep for another couple of hours.

'Marsha', she said rubbing her eyes and creeping closer towards me, 'I think it's time we thoroughly investigated the other murders and determined precisely who these victims were. For instance, the one in Liverpool wasn't named in the newspaper. All they said was "prostitute."'

'See your point Maeve. That stuck in my mind too. I'm thinking the same way. I don't actually know anyone living in Liverpool though. Mike's mum went to live there but course you know he hasn't heard a word in some months now. I told him that after this case is solved I'll look into it for him and find his mum...' My voice trailed off. My conversation in the morning is boring and wanes quickly because I can't be bothered to talk until I've had my caffeine. An overwhelming anxiety swept over me all the same. At the back of my mind I knew what Maeve was getting at; knew exactly where she was coming from, but I couldn't face it. It didn't matter. Maeve gnawed at problems, like a dog with a bone. She could think laterally too. I think I knew what was coming next.

'Marsha, you know, I've had a good look at Mike. He has an oriental look about him. Don't you think so?'

'Of course he bloody well has Maeve. His mother is bloody well Chinese!! Didn't I say Maeve? Didn't I say?' I shouted like a first-class bitch.

'No you didn't Marsha.' She spoke one hundred and fifty decibels softer than my embarrassing outburst. She remained calm and held her voice in the same soft monotone.

'All I wanted to say was, that the one we've just mentioned, the prostitute from Liverpool, well, that print wasn't clear at all. On the other hand, you could tell that the woman was pretty and if I'm not mistaken she had rather slanted eyes.'

'God Maeve! How did I know you were going to say something stupid like that? Now stop! That has to be the most preposterous statement you've made to date!' I was angry, frustrated, exasperated and upset at the very idea.

I had realised earlier that the possibility of the "pretty woman with the slanted eyes," being Mike's mother, was a real one. All the same I was out of order.

'Maeve. I'm so sorry! I shouldn't have vented my anger at you....' I whimpered screwing a tea towel up into the shape of a hangman's noose.

'Not another word dearie.' Lordy, she could be so patronising. 'Of course, you don't want it to be true. Supposing, just supposing, that the Liverpool prostitute... no stop waving your hands around and tutting, hear me out...supposing she happened to be Mike's mother who for some reason led a double life. She certainly wouldn't have been the first to resort to such lengths if she needed the money. In addition to that, supposing Ed Prescotte discovered her secret ... well? And what of Lockburn – he was on to something!'

My toast dropped heavily on to the china plate. My hair drooped sadly into my eyes and I slumped on to a kitchen chair a defeated woman.

'But Maeve,' I started, 'she was blonde and petite just like the others, surely a Chinese woman would have jet black straight hair like Mike's.'

What a feeble statement that appeared to be, especially from my so-called radical-thinking brain. It was painfully obvious, to Maeve, that anyone could use any kind of disguise, these days. It wasn't that long ago we were discussing the common use of coloured contact lenses and wigs. They were fantastic nowadays. Who the devil was I kidding? Maeve was right. The subject should be up for investigation professionally. I allowed these thoughts to roam around my mind but only for seconds, as I had to halt them quickly. They'd created palpitations and a cold sweat throughout my body. I shivered - I was scared! Scared for Mike and scared for Kerri. What if all this was true? What if Mike got wind of it? What if Mike and Kerri confronted Prescotte?

'Marsha where's Bill? Still in Bed?'

'No Maeve,' I sighed wistfully, 'he's on "earlies" for three days.'

'So he'll be at the station then?'

'Yes he will. I'd better ring him.'

I rang through to the station but Bill had set off for an overnight stay in Hampshire. He hadn't wanted to wake me up too early to tell me that, so he'd conveniently left a message at the station's enquiry desk asking them to ring me after nine-thirty.

'Does he have his mobile with him by any chance? Would you know a thing like that? He normally switches it off and leaves it...'

She cut me off midstream to tell me...

'...It's actually on his desk. I can see straight through to his office from here. His door's wide open and there's a mobile perched upright on his filing cabinet.'

'Oh no! Is that Anthea?'

'Yes it is. Is this D I Lines's wife – as if I didn't know?' she half-laughed.

'It is. Look, Anthea, could you take my mobile number down?' I had to rack my brains here. How many times do I ring myself to be able to memorise my own number? Finally I dredged it up from my subconscious and asked her to phone a message through to Bill's destination, asking him to try me on my mobile at the first opportunity.

'Thanks love.' I rang off and turned to face Maeve again. Not a pretty sight!

'Marsha? Why don't you and I go over to Liverpool and perhaps stay over for a day? On a fact finding mission as it were. What do you say? We'll give our charges another half hour before we wake them; tell them we've some P.I. work today that will take us over to Liverpool. We'll come home late tomorrow afternoon but while we're there we'll have time to try a trace on Mike's mother. It won't be a lie will it? What's to lose? If I'm right you'll save Bill a job, waiting for the Liverpool Police to ever get started. Missing persons are not a priority in Liverpool City. Their crime rate is phenomenal. Come on Marsha. What do you say?'

Well how could I resist the Alsatian grin?

'I say I think you're absolutely right Maeve. Let's have a quick breakfast and walk Jenks. Can't go without him, now can we?'

'Gosh no! He may turn out to be star of the show,' Maeve quipped at the huge alert chocolate face ogling back at her.

Having procured the relevant address from Mike, we allowed him and Kerri to escape back into their dreams. I stuck a message for Hetta on to a kitchen cupboard door so that she wouldn't miss it. I didn't want her worrying about our whereabouts, or rather whether we were eating properly or not whilst out of her sight.

96

We were on our way! I had my A-Z tucked in my jacket pocket and consulted it many times. Helpful though it was, I still had loads of problem navigating to Anglo Terrace. In my wisdom, I had persuaded Maeve that we shouldn't need books to find It. It must surely be in the vicinity of the Anglican Cathedral. But I was wrong! No such luck! After another hour and a half, we found Anglo Terrace in a broken down back street. Number sixteen looked positively horrendous from the outside. The upstairs windows had curtains but not so the downstairs. Trundling around to the back, I would have sworn it was the stage prop for Steptoe and Son. What with rubbish bags strewn from here to Kingdom come, old garden ornaments half buried, it was a complete wreck of a garden with only the occasional head of a gnome signifying its partial burial by the five-feet high grass.

It displayed features that indicated a once colourful, well-kept garden, particularly after sighting overgrown herbs, riotous lavender and the heads of daffodils peeping out of dense tumbling piles of weeds. This tangled profusion staked more than its claim as it visibly oppressed apple mint that had gone completely wild. Intermingled with all that, a choking peony acted out its last throes.

The broken down back door invited us nervous explorers to enter and look around. It appeared that either squatters had lived here or were living here. It stupidly crossed my mind that this was the sort of place Hetta would love to blitz. We strode over piles of rusty empty food cans and beer cans, then had to listen to a running tap that had refused to bend to my will and be turned off. No furniture decorated the dusty, stained floors of this desolate and forlorn room, so we looked upstairs. In the larger of the bedrooms, the same mess repeated itself. Only a large photograph caught my attention - then another and then three more, until finally a poster with the header, Jasmine – Porn Queen.

'Maeve! Look hard at this lot!' I gasped.

'I'm looking Marsha! I'm looking!'

We rifled around the myriad of photos and papers. Maeve came up with a real bonanza. She held a photograph in a broken and battered frame. It showed a beautiful Chinese woman nestling into the shoulder of a man looking at her longingly. The man being Eddie Prescotte! It was right that Maeve found it and not me. I know I would have dropped it like a hotcake and it would have completely shattered. We had an empty briefcase with us, to carry our findings. Maeve carefully placed handfuls into it; torn ones, whole ones, halves and quarters. Then she saw it.An album that I had missed had not escaped Maeve's keen eye. She retrieved it and squashed that into the briefcase too.

In the meantime I'd ventured to look at the photo frame and took the photo out. Turning it over I read: *Lucy and Eddie -1981*. I shoved it into Maeve's hand to put into the case with the rest of them. It was me who then shot Maeve a horrified look after placing two pictures side by side, one of Lucy Prescotte, one of Jasmine. It didn't take a Sherlock Holmes to see that they were one and the same person. I felt the tears sting my cheeks, more in disbelief than grief. I cried for Mike, for Kerri and for Eddie Prescotte, only tears would not help. I had some heavy investigating to attend to, both here and at

Liverpool Police Station. Maeve proffered a friendly hand on my arm.

'Come on girl. You're made of stern stuff. You'll ride this. Let's start with the neighbours. Go and get Jenks out of the car. That's it! Dry your eyes.'

It was obvious that the house next door was uninhabited with its shuttered up doors and windows. There would be no one there to question. We moved on to the next one. It was a scruffy looking but passable habitation. We knocked and waited. A voice shouted,

'Bog off! We don't want any!'

We knocked again.

'You deaf? Get lost! If yer Jehovah's Witnesses I'll 'ave ya,' the gruff voice threatened.

'Young man. I am a solicitor. I would merely like you to assist me with my enquiries regarding a tenant at number sixteen.'

As no immediate answer came forth, Maeve threw in an incentive. 'If you can be of help there may be a small financial reward in it for you.'

She winked at me, or rather, blinked, as I felt both of my own eyebrows furrow and knit together. Nonetheless, it did have the desired effect.

The door opened. I can truthfully say I have never seen anything like it before in my life. It was a man, possibly in his late twenties, early thirties, with hair as long as Methuselah accompanied by a growth of beard not far behind his hair length. I would not say either, that the checked lumberjack shirt was exactly on his back, more balancing on his shoulders. He smelt rather like stewed cabbage too. The worse thing of all had to be the scratching and pulling of his skin, which told me his body hair, was probably a playground for a multitude of lice. His trousers may have been grey once upon a time but they held so much grease I'd be hard pushed to give a valid colour description. To top it all a lengthy piece of dirty rope held them up masterfully. My eyes still shifting downwards, I studied black plimsolls that must have seen better days many moons ago.

'Come in the pair of ya. Take a seat,' he said transferring rubbish from two kitchen chairs, swiftly depositing from one to another,

'Well! Ge'r on with it then!' he said impatiently but swiftly changed his tune. In all likelihood, he'd remembered there would be monetary gain if he complied. 'My name's Jim by the way. Jim Ryder.'

Maeve led the way.

'Thank you so much for inviting us in, Jim. My name's Maeve. This is my good friend and colleague, Private Investigator Marsha Riordan. Now we won't take much of your time Jim. We'd like to know if you've had any dealings with the lady who lived next door but one at number sixteen?'

'Oh you mean Jasmine, the Porno, alias Lucy the sweet gel?' he asked reasonably politely.

'Well yes! Can you tell us anything?'

'I can tell you 'most everything 'bout 'er. Where do you want me to start?'

'Well from when you first knew her,' I pressed home,

excited at the prospects of something solid at last.

'Ya know she's dead don't ya?'

We gave a quick nod.

'Bloody shame.' He turned towards his worn out broken-down cooker and ruminated. 'She was a lovely woman ya know an' don't let anyone tell you different. Used to talk ta me lots she did our Lucy. Her people stayed back in China. 'Er dad died two years ago and 'er mum got really down. She wanted to come over 'ere to Lucy but didn't 'ave the fare see. Lucy 'ad made good y'know; a schoolteacher. Trouble was 'er ole man used to take all 'er wages. Gambling man. Bet you didn't know that did ya?'

My heart sank as I thought of the only side to Ed Prescotte that I knew. He was such a handsome, quiet, polite man, who helped practically all the neighbourhood. This would prove a difficult time for me let alone Mike.

'We know nothing about her or her family, really Jim, anything will help. Keep going.' I said, hoping he would continue as affably as he'd begun. I desperately needed a coffee but who knew what manner of nasty bugs lurked in the kitchen. We let him rattle on with his tale. His habit of scratching had already affected Maeve who tried discreetly to scratch the back of her head with her pencil. She'd got me at it now. My forefinger gradually forced its way up my sleeve.

'So ya see,'cos the old man took all her money and 'er old mum living on 'er own near destitute she was desperate. She knew she 'ad the looks and the body so she started to sell 'erself, poor old love. I'll tell yer somethin' else. Do

101

ya know every night she came in, she used to pray, for doin' them things with men. All 'cos of that bastard of an 'usband. Savin' to get her mum over she was but then she would 'ave 'ad ta find 'er somewhere to live an' all. 'E wouldn't 'ave 'er 'ere. An then there was the boy. Michael I think she called 'im; beautiful child, good-natured. She wanted the best for 'im. How's 'e copin' wiv 'is mum's death like?'

'He doesn't know yet,' Maeve croaked pedantically forcing herself to keep control.

'Bloody 'ell! Ain't that the pits!'

'So what do you know of her husband Jim?' He threw his empty tobacco packet down and reached for a new one from his cluttered cupboard top. Then he proceeded to roll a perfectly, cylindrical cigarette between his dirty podgy fingers.

'Not that much really. Oilrigs is what 'e's used to. Big money there ya know! Then 'e 'ad 'is accident like. Did 'is back in, so 'e says. Couldn't lift a shopping bag at one time. 'Ow is he anyway?'

'Okay.' I said not wanting to say something that could be repeated.

'Well I think it's a bloody great shame she 'ad to resort to going on the game. That's the top and bottom of it ladies. Now I reckon that's worth twenty quid of anybody's money. What do you reckon?'

Maeve reluctantly pulled thirty pounds, not twenty, out of her wallet and placed it on a tiny manufactured space on the kitchen table.

'Much obliged ta ya ladies' he said gleefully. 'Come

102

again anytime. Now I must ask ya ta leave 'cos I'm putting the radio on. Horses ya see. My race starts in about six minutes.'

'Thank you very much for all your help Jim. I shouldn't think we'll need to see you again but you never know do you?'

He saluted as he closed the door behind us.

'What did you think to that lot Marsha?'

'H'm, considering that he knew he would be paid for his trouble he could have been telling us the absolute truth or an embroidered half-truth or simply a pack of lies. Personally, I thought he was speaking the truth. He had no reason to lie. Not only that, he gave the impression that he really liked Lucy Prescotte didn't he?'

'Yes, I feel the same way, but what you think about this business of Prescotte working on the oilrigs and damaging his back Marsha? It certainly isn't apparent by the way he throws his spade about is it?'

'No it isn't. That thought crossed my mind straight away. In fact he's as strong as an ox. Now Maeve, none of this indicates that Eddie is the murderer does it? I mean he could be just as much the victim...

'...Whoa ...hold it right there Marsha.' I could almost see Maeve's mind working overtime on this. 'He does have the motive though doesn't he?'

'Yes for sure he does but Ed never goes out of the area.'

'And how would you know that? Come on, let's find Liverpool Police Station.'

We were about to set off when my mobile buzzed. It was Bill, an irate Bill, asking what the hell did I think I was doing. I wish he'd stop worrying about me so that I could follow my leads. Having uttered soothing words to my spouse, he succumbed to being helpful. He said he would contact Liverpool Police and tell them what we'd found. If we sat tight, he would ring us straight back with details of all the red-light districts. He thought we might as well put our time in trying to find any prostitutes who actually knew Lucy as Jasmine of course!

Maeve and I took advantage of the lull and sat with the windows wound down to give ourselves some fresh air after Jim's sour kitchen. Jenko was wide-awake now. I'm sure he knows Bill's voice and listens in to our conversations. He certainly did a great deal of wagging and shaking when Bill and I were talking.

It can't have been more than six minutes, when Bill rang me back with the relevant information. His tone had changed. He was in fact pleased with our find. We promised to keep all our photographs safe and bring them home the next day.

However, hunger now dictated our next half-hour of activity. We found what looked like a reputable restaurant and ate a light meal. It was after all, six thirty now. Plotting our next moves, Maeve suggested we book into a small hotel or a Bed and Breakfast.

'Whichever we see first,' I said. 'We won't have time to try them out as we've some footwork to do.' We didn't have to look far. Ten minutes drive found us at a set of traffic lights, waiting on red. We both browsed to the right and left of the street while we waited for green. Maeve spotted a small hotel to her right, The Black Horse.

Unfortunately we had to go the full length round the ring road and double back to find the entrance but the choice seemed a pretty decent one. Not a large building but it would be adequate for our needs. After all, it was a bed for a night and breakfast in the morning. We signed the register and toddled off to our room for a quick shower and coffee.

We sipped our coffee and made an effort to relax for five minutes. No such luck! Angry muffled voices that at first seemed to come from the landing, disturbed us. In no time at all we realised that the voices, now raised, were coming from the room next door.

'Doesn't look like we'll have much sleep tonight Maeve. Sounds like a lover's tiff next door.'

Having released the last word from my mouth, we heard a loud thud and a soft moan. This saw us both shoot out of our room and bang like fury on their door. It opened in a flash and a young man ran out with blood on his hands.

'Hey you come back here!' Maeve shouted after him.

'No bloody chance lady!'

CHAPTER TEN

'Dear God love, you're such a tiny thing to take a beating like this. What on earth's been going on in here?' I said helping the poor young woman on to the bed. She had a head wound and a cut on her arm. As they were only superficial, we managed to sponge her down and wrap her in a blanket to help with the shock. Maeve picked up the telephone and asked for an outside line to ring the police. With that the young woman shot up and pleaded with Maeve to stop. Her pure, light blue eyes engaged with mine, hoping that I would help her out here.

'Okay, hold it Maeve. Best put the thing down,' I said in an effort to appease. I turned to the young woman who looked no older than early twenties and asked why we shouldn't contact the police.

'They won't do anything,' she stammered out, much more subdued. 'They never helped poor Jasmine when she was plagued with a stalker. Now she's dead. If I don't get out of this city, I will be too.'

'Why did that man attack you?' I asked quietly.

'Because I only do straight sex and he's a "pervy."' She saw me catch Maeve's eye again and went on to say. 'Don't look like that at one another. I have to earn a living somehow. I've a young'un to feed. So, I'm a prostitute. All right?'

'Hey, look, before we go any further young lady, your profession is your own business. It would be difficult for us to have ignored you when a man has just done this to you and we've heard it all. Besides that, you may be able to help us.'

Before she had the chance to ask how, I watched Maeve whip out a clean handkerchief from her stout black handbag and had pick up a stiletto knife from the now stained white rug, beside the dressing table.

'Well now Marsha, what have we here?'

'It looks like a stiletto to me Maeve.'

The young woman looked at it and turned away cringing, gently caressing her throat with both hands.

'Nearly did for me didn't he?' she whimpered.

'Yes but you are all right. You've had a narrow escape. Now, what's your name?'

'My working name is Lily. My real name is Janet.'

'Tell me Janet, what do you know of Jasmine, the beautiful Chinese woman? Her real name is Lucy Prescotte. We came here on behalf of her teenage son. She's been missing for months. We had hoped we'd be taking her back with us but discovered that she was murdered.'

'Does her son know she's dead?'

'No, not yet. Please - how much do you know about Jasmine?'

She started to cry. Maeve reached for the small kettle to make her a warm drink. I put my arm around Janet's shoulder and wiped away the smudged mascara from her cheeks. I wanted to show her we were friends. I wanted to encourage her to talk.

'All the men liked Jasmine.' she started. 'She was a lovely woman. All the working girls got on with her well too.

She earned fabulous money, especially with her porn films. She never saw us girls stuck. Not for food or clothes if we needed them. She even stopped the pimps from muscling in.'

'The pimps? She managed to stop them?' I gasped in disbelief 'Did any of them threaten her at all? In a serious way I mean?'

'Yes,' she paused reluctantly, 'there was one who stalked her. It started about four months ago. Big guy he was. Stood bout six feet five or six - totally besotted with her he was. Wanted her all to himself. Sent her flowers, notes. Left messages on her phone. Always hanging around.'

'This is a long shot I know Janet but I don't suppose she left any of her stuff with you did she?' I asked, with my fingers crossed behind me.

'Funny you should say that. She left almost all of her stuff with me. It's back at my place.... here... who are you anyway? What are you asking all these questions for? Who did you say you were?'

'Janet I'm a professional Private Investigator. My niece has been going out with Lucy's son for two and a half years now. I promised to help him find his mum. Maeve is a friend of mine, out for a ride with me. We're from the Hull area.' I didn't think the time was right to say that Maeve was a solicitor and I was married to a Detective Inspector.

'Why would Lucy leave all her private things with you Janet?'

'Well, we were mates you see. We almost always had the same clients. The odd one was okay but most of them she didn't trust. She didn't want them going into her private things, like her letters. Then she used to tell me about this nightmare she had ever so often. She dreamt that her punters had found her son's address, or her husband's and that they'd blackmail her. You know, making her give them all the money she earned or they would write to her family and tell them what kind of life she was leading. That kind of thing – you know what I'm saying. Often she'd wake up screaming. She was lovely though. As good inside as she looked outside. God knows why she couldn't find something different to do. Anyway we were mates. She trusted me - that's why she hid everything at my place – in case hers got turned over.'

'Would you let us take them now? We'll be discreet as to what photographs reach her son and we'll destroy the rest.'

'I dunno. I don't know you from Adam do I? How do I know you're who you say you are?'

'Look Janet, I wasn't going to mention it but my husband is a Detective Inspector. No, don't look like that,' I said hurriedly, as her eyes rolled like glass marbles. 'We will protect you. Don't worry. But Lucy's belongings are far safer with us. Now - what do you think? Pick up the phone Janet. Ring who you like. Check me out as much as you need to,' I said confidently, hoping she'd believe me.

'Don't have much choice do I?' she moaned sullenly.

'You do Janet. We certainly wouldn't take them by force and you can choose which photographs of Lucy, you'd like to keep for yourself. How's that sound?' By the looks of her dubious expression and her fiddling with her hair, I suppose the offer didn't sound that good but there wasn't a better option for her, than us. She eventually settled for that.

'Yes, okay. I hope I can trust you to do the right thing. I think I can.'

'That's the spirit girl! Now, would you like us to order you a meal from room service? We've eaten but I'm sure Maeve and I can stand another coffee whilst you eat.' She almost threw us a smile.

After she'd eaten and downed a double whisky, we all piled into our car to go back to Janet's flat. Maeve had placed the stiletto knife inside a polythene bag and carefully tucked it away in a side pocket of her large handbag. We'd get back to that later. On the way, we asked her if she knew the name of her attacker.

'Oh yes!' she said with a start. 'We all know that headcase – try to keep him at arm's length. Only - he never came at me with a knife before!'

'Big chap though, from what we managed to glimpse as he ran?'

'Yeah. Bit scary sometimes. Wish I could get off the game. I'd give anything to get out of this. You never know from one day to the next what's going to happen to you. What is the next bloke going to want you to do for him? I'm so ashamed of my self, honest! If my old mum knew she'd kill me herself.'

'Do you really want to get out of it Janet? Because if you do, we can help you, properly I mean.'

Her face lit up like a firework display!

'Do you really mean it Miss?'

'Yes we really mean it.' Maeve and I sang back at her. This notion definitely lifted her spirits. I took note of her appearance as I drove. I glanced up at my mirror as often as I could. I observed a strange coincidence. She was blonde and a natural one at that: in fact, extremely pretty now that I had a decent look at her. When Maeve and I had originally picked her up from the floor, we realised immediately that she would be described as petite. She fitted the stereotypical woman that was earmarked for these attacks.

'Can you give me a name on this attacker Janet?' I asked, not at all optimistic. When she replied that she could not only name him but she could tell us his age, his address, his shoe size etc. etc. I almost stopped the car. We reached her flat, which was in fact in a respectable area. A first story cottage flat in a part council, part privately owned housing zone, not far from a local chapel. We helped her out and mounted the stairs to her flat that proved to be a miniature palace. I was astounded, probably because I had made assumptions about her: that she may spend all her money on clothes and drugs. This was not the case. Janet it seemed kept an immaculate home. I recognised antique furniture and a couple of good paintings hung over the gas fire area. Moving into the kitchen we saw more of the same, beautifully fitted out in pale blue and yellow and not a pot to be seen. The same carpet of deep red had been fitted throughout. She showed us the bedroom. Not a huge double bed as you'd imagine but a single. The room itself was very simply decorated in pale green to match a dark green carpet and curtains. She laughed at our puzzled faces.

'Not what you expected then? You don't think I bring 'em back here do you? I've got a kid to feed and clothe. That's why I do it. She's at my friends today.

They're off school this week. Got a good mate I have,' she explained without a qualm, that even though she hated the business, when her boyfriend walked out on her she had nothing.

'You ever lived off the Social? Well have you?'

'You don't have to explain yourself Janet and please don't torment yourself either. Now that we are here, let's get to work shall we? If you don't mind me making a few phone calls, I'll get the ball rolling to get some help for you over here.'

'You mean that Miss?'

'Yes I mean it. Now, first things first - please - the name and address of this man who attacked you.'

She had no compunction about supplying all the details about this man. His name was Steve Rodare, aged thirty-two, six feet five, violent with a history of rape and robbery. He had served time for armed robbery and attempted rape. Well that would do for starters. I phoned all this information through to Bill explaining that we were also picking up some documents of Lucy's and perhaps more photographs. The excitement in Bill's voice made him almost inaudible.

'This is it Marsha. We've got him!'

'Oh?' says I. 'How on earth can you be so sure?'

'Well you said that Maeve picked up a stiletto knife?'

'Well - yes?'

'And his form? Marsha this is the killer. He's been roaming all over the country for God knows how long. Stay where you are for at least an hour. I'm going to ring Liverpool Police and have him picked up.

I'll send someone round to pick up the knife. Am I going to have a good sleep tonight? Well done you two.'

'You are that confident Bill. You really think we've nailed him?' I began to enjoy the elation. The excitement infected Maeve too. You'd think we'd won the Lottery! Surely after all this time Eddie Prescotte would be in the clear. Mike would at least have his dad, whatever we'd discovered of his character. Yes, maybe we had found the serial killer. Yet at the back of my mind – I thought, so what if this is the serial killer, here in Liverpool? What about Lockburn's killer – on home ground? I pushed this negative thought to the recesses of my mind, contemplating yes...maybe. Within fifteen minutes of putting the phone down, two uniformed officers were knocking at the door. They explained that Bill had given their office details of Janet's assailant and asked if she would be prepared to attend an identity parade. Although anxious, she agreed, if Maeve and I could go too.

The Police took their leave and promised, as always, they'd be in touch. In the meantime I rang all the relevant authorities to find out as much as I could about helping Janet on the road to recovery and a change of lifestyle. She looked pale a wan: her eyes large and staring from shock and fear.

'You know that if I do this thing I'll have to move town?' she said looking down, studying her shoes. Her long blonde, wispy hair hung sweetly, framing a pretty elfin-shaped face, now that it had seen a brush.

'No worries, we'll sort it. Trust me, eh?' I said, doing my damnedest to instil some confidence whilst at the same time wondering how many times she'd heard that one before.

I asked if we could make her another cup of tea. It doesn't solve problems but we all do it in times of stress. She murmured a yes, so I told Maeve to sit down, it was my turn. However, Maeve was in no mood for sitting. Instead she offered to walk and water Jenks. Standing in the kitchen, I felt flat somehow as though this case, although it looked close to being solved, wasn't finished at all. What if this man had alibis for the other murders? What if he didn't? Either way his arguments would be slim with his previous record.

There was a mirror standing on the window ledge. I peered into it. I knew that I looked well, so what was it behind my eyes. What was it that lurked provokingly? Was it only anti-climax, that life could perhaps steer back on track. It must be imagination, of which I have a particularly vivid one. Yes, maybe we could tie this one up. I crossed my fingers yet again and hoped. We'd have to wait and see.

Bill made good his journey from Hampshire to Liverpool. Was he a sight for sore eyes? It felt as though I hadn't seen him for a year. Jenks went crazy wild as soon as he set eyes on Bill. He bowled him over. Nothing, but no one could get anywhere near or between Bill's body and the chocolate beast, so obviously devoted to my partner! We scuttled through the city centre after a small shopping spree with Maeve, Janet and Jenks in tow. To outsiders we could have been mistaken for holidaymakers – tourists or the like. As for Maeve, she had the enormous task of walking Jenks on his lead. He had always shown dislike to being leashed but remained obedient because he liked Maeve; she fussed him up so much. As if to say "thank you" or "you can give me lots of treats today", he stuck out his chest and held his broad, proud head forward. Bill hugged me and squeezed me like on our early dates while we indulged in animated conversation.

'They've picked him up Marsha.' He said, pecking my cheek and stroking my hair as we walked.

'Already? Wow! Don't let grass grow under their feet do they?'

'It would be good Marsha, if this were the man responsible for it all. That last murder was a bit too close to home for my liking. Liverpool is far out. Driffield is close to us.'

'Well, leave it alone for a while Bill, can't you? Where are we heading for anyway?'

'Well, I'd like you and Maeve to go back home. Check in at the station and ask for Helen Wright. She has a safe house organised for Janet and her child. Police Officers will take her out there as soon as she's done the Identification Parade. A friendly face might be appreciated.'

'That's great!'

'So ... I'm sorry to have to leave you but I'm going back to Liverpool Police Station to sit in on the interview with this head case ...and before you ask, no you can't join me.'

I stopped in my tracks and turned to face him. 'You'll be home as soon as you can Bill? I'm missing you.'

In the middle of the street he took my face in his hands and kissed me so gently it meant the world to me.

'Miss you too lovely lady. Don't worry I'll bring a copy of the taped interview home with me. Hey and Marsha, you've done one hell of a good job here. See you later sweetheart.'

CHAPTER ELEVEN

Six months passed by swimmingly after the trial of Steve Rodare. I lay awake one night waiting for Bill to come home. It must have been elevenish. My magazines were not interesting. My novels were boring. I could not concentrate on reading, sleeping, knitting or any of the things that usually help me off to sleep when Bill is working late. He would be home by two in the morning if he were lucky. I'd played the tape again this evening. I had listened to the interview tape so many times I practically knew it verbatim. Something didn't add up. At the trial Rodare admitted to all counts but two. He swore blind that he didn't kill Lucy Prescotte or Lockburn. Logical? What's more, Bill and I read so much information on Lucy's murder we almost missed something vital. Lucy may have lived in Liverpool, yet her body had actually been found in Driffield. Forensics also supported the theory that she was murdered in Driffield.

Now as far as the Public at Large was concerned, Steve Rodare was responsible for the killings, the rapes and all the attacks, even the ones in Hull. They pinned the lot on him. What were the police to think? This man had after all, confessed with pride to other murders, whilst emphatically denying the remainder. Either he was the perpetrator using a repeated copycat style as a gross trademark, or, someone had copied *him*.

The psychiatrist present at the trial had assessed him to be psychopathic. So it seems to them that they may in fact have caught the murderer of all of these dastardly crimes or they may not. Was there another psycho on the loose?

Mike took his mother's death badly.

'I'll kill him if nobody else will,' he'd screamed in court. 'Why should he be in jail alive when my mother is dead?' He had to be forcibly taken out of court, as one would imagine. Afterwards his GP sedated him. Did Rodare kill Lucy or not? She had been found in a scruffy bedsit in Driffield. Her body had been cleaned to an immaculate state and wrapped in a clean single sheet. This murder was all the more strange because there was not a clean piece of linen to be had in the bedsit. On the other hand, Eddie Prescotte showed no sign of emotion in court. The judge praised him for his self-control. He thought he was being extremely brave for his son. Bill was praised for his part and so was I.

Maeve took a holiday in Corfu for three weeks and I went back to work with Jenks. So why do I have this frightful feeling of "something's-about-to-happen"? I should have confided something to Bill yesterday only I put it down to a foolish prank. My underwear has gone missing off the clothesline. It's never happened before so I'm trying not to let it bother me too much.

Mike and his dad came to tea. Kerri joined us of course. Before all of these murders occurred, Eddie was always happy and jokey. Now he's totally subdued. It's knocked the stuffing out of him. His conversation was stilted, you could say boring too. There was no light in his eye. The main problem with that evening was that Ed never took his eyes off me. The look in them bothered me. Hidden hostility is what came into my mind. I kept Jenks by my legs under the table the whole time. I think Ed will need a psychiatrist soon if he doesn't snap out of it. He appeared to change when the subject of the trial came up as we chin-wagged around the table.

Everyone except me, said they breathed a sigh of relief when Rodare was sentenced but I did not and I told everyone so. I became adamant at our teatime discussion that I believed there was a murderer on the loose, that Rodare could be doing time for. That was when Ed stopped eating for a moment, a noticeable moment, and glared at me. Bill observed but held his silence. I thought I'd give the tape one more re-run as soon as our guests had left. I could almost memorise the speech word for word:

"...You'll not pin 'em all on me bloody coppers I was trying to make a name for myself see. Deserved it anyway, bloody prossies. But not that one in Driffield mate. No way. Can't pin that on me. I told you where I was. I was in bloody Holland all Bank Holiday. That you can check out - but you won't will ya?..."

Of course, I thought him a psycho-pervert. He'd gone over to the land of liberation, free love, legal red light district and all that, I'll bet! But if the police wouldn't' check it, I would *and* first thing in the morning!

It was a lovely August morning as Jenks and I walked to my office. It was warming to be able to nod to the various characters that smiled harmoniously, acknowledging me on my way to work. Never knowing their names made it doubly pleasant, somehow civilised. It gave me a feeling of joie de vivre. Jenks picked the feeling up too. He seemed to wag and smile at passers by as I looked down admiring his rich glossy coat reflecting the early morning sunlight.

I loved going to my office, having my own space, my own business. It looked impressive from the outside. A glamorous fascia board in blue and white read "Marsha Riordan - Private Investigator."

I unlocked the door pushing the letters back on doing so. Before I picked them up I toddled around to the side wall where there happened to be a special hatch for Jenks to come and go as he pleased. It allowed him access to the grassed area on the grounds of the local community centre and back again. It is an ingenious creation, purpose built.

There is an area of porch for him large enough for a basket and a water dish. A small passageway leads out from here that lets him straight onto the Common. I always bolted the large hatch down before going home in the evening and it became the first ritual to perform when I came back to the office in the mornings. Fashioned in the same way as a cat-flap only larger, Jenks got the hang of it right away. He's so clever that when I first had it done he spent almost an hour messing around coming and going out of it. It comes in extremely handy. If irate clients raise their voices or bang a fist on my counter, up comes this massive head together with a massive growl. Does the trick every time.

I filled Jenk's dish with fresh water and peeled a banana for him. Yes I spoil him but he is partial to a little fruit. He wolfed it down in one gulp and slurped a drink leaving his jowls dripping like a fountain. I tried to tear my unbelieving eyes away from him and settle down to open the mail. I peeped from the corner of my eye and watched him naturally arrange himself comfortably in his basket. We both then shared a heaving sigh of contentment.

The first ten or so envelopes contained cheques and thank you letters for "a job well done", which always put a feather in my cap! A letter from Maeve also added brightness to my morning, asking when we could meet up for lunch or could she come round to dinner for more of Hetta's cooking. That request was easy! I picked up the phone. Maeve answered it.

'And what is it you'd like to eat at my place my friend?' I asked laughing.

'Marsha! Lovely to hear from you my dear. Do you know I've actually missed you and your family,' she gushed down the phone.

'What a charming thing to say Maeve. Feel free to join us tonight. I'll ring Hetta now. She'll be thrilled.'

'Are you sure it's all right at such short notice?'

'Of course Maeve, you're welcome any time all. You know that.'

'That's settled then. Seven o'clock okay?'

'Splendid.' I replied.

Having sorted that out, I skimmed my eyes over my mail quickly, noting that the remainder of the envelopes were utility and stationary bills. That small task also out of the way, I made my first coffee of the morning. My next job was to trawl through my private directory of European contacts. I'd addressed the problem of Rodare's denial of Lucy's murder and needed to settle in my own mind his whereabouts at the time of her murder. I found a Belgium phone number of a dear friend of mine, an ex policeman who, too, had his own P.I. business.

He made an extremely popular port of call because he looked and acted like the fictional Hercule Poirot: an extremely clever little man. I related a potted story over the phone, furnished him with names and dates and asked him to track down Steve Rodare's movements from the days leading up to and after Lucy's murder.

He blew kisses down the phone promising to fax me after two o'clock that afternoon. Well pleased with myself, I brought the computer to life and proceeded to catch up on letters to prospective clients who had written asking for appointments. I could phone them all but I thought it much better to send appointments through like all other professional bodies, e.g. the hospital. By eleven I'd completed outstanding filing, cleaned up the office and opened up the appointment book. A client for missing persons was due at one forty-five. A divorced client who desperately needed information to prove her ex had committed adultery for the whole of the duration of the marriage had arranged to see me at three. Between four and five I'd arranged to go into college to give a lecture on the laboriousness of crime detection. That meant I'd have a comparatively easy day's work.

The doorbell buzzed me back into this world. Because the front door of my office opened straight onto the street, it was permanently and securely locked. This enabled me to manage my work without any old body throwing the door open and interrupting my time with clients. Although I had a separate interview room, it served as part of my security system. Bill had made sure I had a sophisticated modus operandi throughout, as I held confidential information. It worked. Although Jenko protects me wherever I am, the office is empty during the night, which is when the system goes into play.

The buzz had to be my morning bacon butty. I should not indulge like this but I do all the time! Sometimes I feel guilty blaming Hetta for feeding us so well but I am as big a culprit. I pressed the relevant button after checking my spy hole, allowing Gail to breeze in smiling.

'Morning Marsha. That'll be one pound twenty please love. Business good?' she asked, slapping the butty down on my desk, missing a bundle of important papers by a millimetre.

'Couldn't be better Gail, thanks love.' I chirped back, fumbling in my purse for change.

'Can't stay to chat this morning, girl. Got a queue a mile long. See you tomorrow.'

'Bye Gail and thanks,' I shouted as she slammed the door behind her. Jenko smelt the bacon and waddled through. We always shared this treat. It made me feel better if I didn't eat a whole one to myself. The only problem was, Jenko never put excess weight on. He used boundless energy exercising and chasing balls when we walked through the park. However I dismissed the weight problem, deciding to pull my accounts up to date on the computer at the same time as enjoying my butty. Any nutritionist would tell me that this is bad for me. Then again - so is being shot at! I live dangerously.

My monthly spreadsheet began to churn itself out when the door buzzed again. Before I had chance to open the door, loud voices seemingly in panic mode, alerted Jenks so that he barked furiously. Yet, we both knew those voices.

The first tear-stained face to appear was Kerri's. Looking over her shoulder was Mike.

'Oh no, you two - now what!' I bellowed, ushering them through into my private interview room.

'Dad's gone Marsha. He's disappeared!' Poor Mike moaned.

'What! How do you know? I mean could he have gone to visit relatives?

'No, no! He's never done anything like this before! He's so depressed. So down, it's unbelievable.' This unkempt young man was extremely worried.

'Does Bill know?' I asked tentatively.

'Yes, we rang him at the station. It looks like dad's been gone well over twenty-four hours. I feel terrible. While I've been staying over here he's done nothing in the house. There are pots in the sink and his clothes are strewn all over the place. You know, as if he's not been bothered about anything. Our house stinks – it's bloody atrocious! I really thought he'd be okay now, Marsha. That's why I've stayed on for so long at your place with Kerri. Didn't think I had to worry about dad anymore.'

'Now look you two, don't panic. No news is good news.'

'We know all that Aunt Marsha. We can't help but worry. He can't be well, can he? He can't be right. He's probably been like this since the trial and we haven't noticed. We didn't know that something could be wrong.' Kerri churned out miserably, her voice trembling.

'Okay, okay.' I tried to soothe them, quite unsuccessfully. 'I want you to go back home and wait for me. I'll see if I can think of something. I have some clients to meet today. Go home and try to relax. Have you both caught up with your studies?'

'Yes we have.' Kerri said on her way out, managing to keep a poker-straight face. It was such a fib! I remember being a student myself. At any rate they seemed mildly placated. I rummaged out the file I would need for my next client. I still had at least an hour and a half to kill. I rang Bill who confirmed the problem. He explained that there was not a great deal to be done as regards searching for him, as he wasn't a minor. But he would circulate a description among his men and ask that they keep an eye out. He told me not to worry too much but to get on with my own work and he would see me later. He also thought that the idea of Maeve coming to dinner would prove an apt distraction.

'Must go Bill. Jenks is barking, something's just tumbled through the letterbox. See you later love. Bye.'

'What's wrong Jenks? Your fur's all up old thing. What are you so cross about?' I said softly stroking his velvety ears as I picked up the offending envelope and tore it open.'

"You next Miss Prim and Proper."

...It read. Now I didn't panic. I'd grown past all that in this job. But I rang Bill back straight away. It would have been hopeless running outside to lay hold of the culprit. They were hardly going to hang around waiting for me to catch them. Bill came right over.

'Well, well, now my lovely wife. Make anything of it yourself?' he said softly, wrapping his arms around me.

'Not a darned thing Bill. Then again, it could be someone related to a client I'm investigating. Can't think of anyone else with a grudge, only perhaps one person.'

Bill sat himself down in my swivel chair and pulled me onto his knee.

'Come on then let's have it. And don't start with, "well I know it sounds stupid but..." Your hunches are always full of promise.' He tugged on one of my arms and kissed my hand. That was to make me talk.

'Well,' I began, 'I'll tell you what's been skulking in the back of my mind. I know you won't think me stupid, I know you better than that, but it's about the serial killer. I still feel in my gut that Rodare was telling the truth about not murdering Lucy. I know he's a psycho but...' Bill opened his mouth to speak but I held up my hand to stop him. 'I think, because my views are no secret, that Lucy's killer would very much like to shut me up once and for all so that his identity can remain anonymous. And let's face it, the police aren't bothered are they, they've locked Rodare away for all of the murders. They don't like loose ends your lot, now do they? Bill, how can he have killed Lockburn? He was nowhere near the area. I've checked   No, someone else murdered Lucy and Lockburn.'

Bill took out his pipe. I knew that he was taking me seriously and putting his thinking head on.

'You know Marsha, I think you could be absolutely right.' My head turned so quickly on hearing this that I pulled my arthritic neck muscles again. I never believed Bill would agree with me so readily on this one.

126

'Really Bill! Sometimes you astonish me!' I said, well pleased with myself. I had reminded him on numerous occasions of my intuition and powers of reasoning.

'I've been none too happy with this case Marsha. Every Police Force works towards an immediate result. They very rarely manage it. Murder cases especially can drag on for months without a decent lead. No, what I dislike about this one is the fact that although Rodare had a foolproof alibi for the time Lucy was murdered, that has not only been deliberately overlooked but the paper work establishing that has gone astray. Despite all the jubilation at Rodare's arrest and conviction, something still sits at the back of my mind that shouts "too obvious". I've tried to shift it from my mind and get on with my work but ... I just don't know...can they all have been wrong? I couldn't discuss any of this with you before for obvious confidentiality of my job sweetheart but it looks as though you're on to it already.'

'Is there a cover up Bill?'

'Well,' he mused, 'I don't think it's something that's been done too covertly. I think it's a case of, "we've got our man, don't let's rock the boat" and after all he was guilty of other murders. So there is no injustice here. "We have results! Wow aren't we a fabulous team!" You know all that macho stuff. But you see unless there is compelling evidence to the contrary, the investigation won't be opened up again.'

'Yes, I see what you mean. Why try to fix something when it isn't broken.'

'That's more it my love but to get back to the problem in hand, has anything else happened to strengthen your feelings on this?' He was stroking and squeezing both my hands by now, so I confessed about my underwear going missing.

I explained that I hadn't bothered mentioning it before because I thought it was a joke. Bill wasn't laughing. His eyes narrowed and up came the angry look reserved for all the baddies.

'Marsha I could not live without you. I love you so much!' I experienced a spontaneous melting as I sank into his arms and we kissed the kiss of young lovers.

'Hey don't worry about me Bill. I will always let you know where I am every minute of the day.' Then Jenks approached of course. He'd trundled into the office when he heard Bill's voice. What a picture the three of us made and what a team! Bill patted the chocolate monster on the head whilst giving him strict instructions not to leave my side, not even for a moment. I felt better for talking to Bill. He too was almost one hundred per cent convinced that a stalker had entered our lives.

'I must get on sweetheart,' I said glancing at my watch, 'I've a client in ten minutes. See you at dinner and don't forget our Maeve is coming over.'

'Yes!' he laughed, thumping his fist into fresh air. He was adorable.

My lecture over at the college, I was pleased that the car park was full and that lots of people were walking back to it in the same direction that I was going. I wondered why Bill hadn't asked to sit in on this lecture in case my stalker was among them. Then I reasoned that I never actually asked him. I normally do and he comes to them when he can. In this instance, he must have known what I suspected and I knew it would come out in the open over dinner.

CHAPTER TWELVE

'My darling Maeve you look wonderful!'

Bill shouted, striding through the hallway. I howled at his antics. Maeve was a wonderful person but she could never look wonderful. If I were a bitchy woman I'd say she resembled a well-groomed German Shepherd but I'm not. I loved her to come over. Bill had made her blush. That was a first. He had also been to the flower shop and purchased two single red roses, one for each of us ladies. I don't think anyone had treated Maeve as a woman before. Her appreciation came shining through her highly creamed and polished face. I loved her too. She was fast becoming one of our favourite people.

It was now a chilly February evening. Hetta had prepared a full beef roast with all the trimmings. As Maeve would stay overnight she could enjoy a couple of drinks with us. I disciplined myself to eat slowly. Medical research shows that you are less inclined to pile weight on if you do this. It was difficult as the beef was so tender and succulent. I wanted my palate to savour the juices big time. Our conversation was companionable, as you would expect. Kerri and Mike were at the pub. Not to drown their sorrows, I must add but merely to take their minds of Ed for a while. Their worrying was not helping anyone. After a good old-fashioned "auntie" talk they'd brightened up. Kerri fancied her chances at the Karaoke as England's answer to Britney Spears. That allowed us to talk freely.

Bill brought up the subject of my stalker and the reasoning behind it all. Maeve placed her knife and fork neatly on her half finished dinner and sipped her wine thoughtfully.

'I'm so pleased you've decided to tell me all this because I am in exactly the same mind - about Rodare not being Lucy's killer.'

That short statement was enough to force Bill and I to drop our knives and forks.

'How's your reasoning working then Maeve?'

'Well. Like Bill, I believe the police have swept certain things under the carpet or at least held over in someone's pending file, as regards Rodare. I mean, for one thing, how can he have been in two places at the same time unless he's discovered how to clone himself. Tell me Marsha, what do you think personally? Have you actually any clue as to who it might be?'

I looked from Maeve to Bill most pensively before committing myself. However, before I could brave the answer, both Bill and Maeve said "Eddie Prescotte!"

'Well, well, well, do we now have three minds that think alike?' I smiled, raising my glass. They reciprocated and we toasted to a resolution.

Bill started first.

'You know Marsha I've never been convinced of Prescotte's innocence from the word go. All the evidence is still there staring us in the face.'

'So why hasn't he been picked up and questioned again Bill?' I quizzed, holding my breath.

'Out of order. Remember the last "shindig" when he took his beating. A big and I mean big investigation is going on there! Not only that, we are having a devil of a job keeping it out of the newspapers. Can you imagine if he is re-arrested, especially for the same crime,

130

they'll have the television cameras zooming in here faster than a rocket launch! Oh no! Then to top it all off, we all know that he's disappeared! What about you Maeve - have you anything to add?'

'All right. What about this? Here's some news that might surprise you. I don't even think Mike knows, otherwise he would surely have boasted about it as youngsters do. I've done some in-depth research, you know inquiries and suchlike and ...I've discovered... that Eddie Prescotte is in fact a PhD. He is a Social Scientist with a specialism in ...guess what?'

'Criminology!' came a hot guess from myself before Bill could blink.

'Right, Marsha!' Maeve replied with massive confidence.

'Oh God!' said Bill, picking up his wine and walking over to the fireplace. He leaned both his arms up against the mantelpiece, thoughtfully placing his wineglass in the middle of it. He studied the half-burned down candlesticks fondly, probably reminiscing one of our romantic dinners. He sighed that awful sigh of the defeated and repeated,

'Oh, God!'

I too must have looked drained after this revelation,

'So,' I murmured into my cupped hands, 'it looks like we've been had! And by a highly intelligent, if corrupt mind.'

'Afraid so.' Maeve looked across. 'Marsha do you remember when Jim, that old neighbour of Lucy's, told us how cruel Prescotte was to Lucy? I actually began to wonder then.'

Yes, me too. But he's never, I mean never exhibited any of those character traits in the time we've known him.'

'But Marsha,' Bill interrupted my thoughts, 'how long have we known him? Has Mike ever witnessed any of this other side? Has he ever said?'

'No I think Kerri would have told us. I'm sure she would have said something.' I threw in, offering my glass up for a refill.' She's a pretty good judge of character for her age and she's stayed over at their place plenty of times. Says Eddie's like a second father to her ... now... he's gone! Nevertheless, Bill, even if we're right I'm certainly not going to stop going about my daily business. Not much point, as all the other attacks or murders took place on Bank holidays. The next one is way off. It's not until Easter.'

'I don't think he'll wait that long Marsha. The longer he leaves it the longer you have to investigate and compile a dossier on him. We police can do nothing unless we have hard evidence that he did kill Lucy or if he attacks you. That's the law ...so ... folks ... what is our game plan? Plus, this time we must hold fast to the idea that he may be pretty damn brilliant which makes him doubly dangerous.' Bill said, pulling his fingers through his hair, trying to be philosophical and calm when all the time he's extremely fearful for my life.

'Let's look on the bright side Bill. As much as this whole saga is distasteful to us all, particularly when at first we all believed Prescotte to be innocent, and he may yet well be but... if it is him, then we need him off the streets before he can kill again. If there is an advantage, in this case at all, it's that we can do plenty of things to avoid risk.

132

I mean all the resources we have from the Police station and not forgetting Jenko!' As I spoke his name, there he was wagging at my feet. 'So the best thing we can do is carry on as normal, being extra vigilant. What do you say Bill?'

'Fine with me but for one thing. I'm going to arrange for WPC Wright to be with you at all times when I'm not around. That means at home, the office, the market - shopping or wherever your P I work takes you. Will you agree to that Marsha?'

'Of course love. She's good company too. When do we implement all this?' I asked Bill. He took no notice. He was on the phone chasing Helen Wright that very minute. Maeve made a point when she explained to Bill and I, that, presuming the killer is Prescotte, he may also make presumptions. For instance that I am taking added precautions as regards my safety and he may well use an accomplice to take me off guard. This made us all look up.

A fundamental point had now been made but one which we might possibly have overlooked.

'And another thing,' Bill chipped in, 'we cannot utter a word of this in front of Kerri and Mike. Agreed?'

'Oh absolutely Bill!' I enthused. 'That goes without saying.'

'But of course!' Maeve barked in a Sergeant Major voice.

On that note, we allowed our evening to take on a more normal tone. Each of us hiding behind our eyes, the terrible things we may have to face.

133

Nine o'clock next morning, Helen breezed in minus her uniform. She propped herself up against the kitchen door, one-foot resting on the spell of the stool, hands in pockets and yelled for coffee.

'I can smell it Marsha. You can always bet on a good coffee at your place!'

'Help yourself Helen I'm putting a load of washing in before I toddle up to the office. Pour me one too please love.'

'Coming up!'

Part of the attraction of Helen's company was the fact that she was a pure no-nonsense woman. She never garbled stupid conversation and always called a spade a spade.

'Are we on our own in the house?' she asked pouring coffee with one hand and refastening a clip into her thick golden tied up locks with the other.'

'Yes, the kids are at college but I'm not entirely happy wherever they are for obvious reasons. You know Helen, for some months now half of me wanted to believe that this whole business was over. The other half niggled about the evidence against Rodare. But it's not over. I'm worried about Mike and Kerri, practically non-stop. I've rung my sister and told her all. Do you know what she said? Talk about "cool". She simply moaned down the phone, "I know what you're like Marsha. Don't be spoiling her. And you can warn Bill, he's even worse." She's great though. She knows the nature of the job. She seemed more concerned about my smoking than the other dangers I bump into. She didn't hang up without a stern admonition about looking after myself though.

Come on Helen, we'll down the coffee and take a nice stroll over to the office.'

We set off with Jenks setting the pace of a brisk walk. As we walked in silence, I glanced at Helen and an ever-so slight bulge was noticeable to my trained eye.

'You packing a gun Helen?'

'Too right I am Marsha. Bill insisted.'

'That's funny, so am I.'

'What?' She threw a mild fit.

'I too am trained in firearms and I have a licence. I haven't told Bill I'm carrying it. He may over-react and become too fearful. If I'm right Helen, this man could kill me anytime anywhere.'

'Point taken Marsha. As it happens I agree with you and I support your actions all the way.'

I felt comfortable now that I'd got that out of the way. On reaching my office door, I half expected to find the office ransacked. But no - all was well. I had also mentioned to Bill, the night before, as we were piling into bed in a rather drunken state, that I was worried about Hetta's safety too. In fact, I was worried about anyone connected to me. I needn't have been. Bill had organised plain-clothes police to watch the house and also to follow the kids everyday over the full twenty-four hours. I could now concentrate on my clients. Jenks settled down to a game of ball in his play area.

Helen agreed to disappear into a room every time a client arrived for an appointment. This way I wouldn't frighten my clients off with my temporary bodyguard. On this particular day everything ticked away like clockwork.

Helen, Jenks and I worked ourselves into our specialised roles. At four o'clock I had seen the last client of the day, and caught up with filing and computer input. So to complete a good day we decided to take Jenks for a good run in the playing fields. Helen and I discussed the possibilities of a girls' night out and how we should book an appointment at the hairdressers to have our hair coloured. Her blonde locks were ready for more highlights and my deep auburn coloured lowlights had practically faded away. After that, we'd go to Alfies for a pizza. We'd make the appointments on arriving back home at my place. That settled, Jenks must have sensed our mood. He could not get away fast enough

We had two rubber balls with us. Helen and I threw them alternately into the thicket to make Jenks work those powerful muscles. Having kept him busy for all of three minutes, Helen and I were about to resume our discussions on hair colour when Jenks came half way back towards us and then stood erect, barking at us. That of course was a signal to me. He had found something. We ran up and followed him into the bushes. Excellently trained, he sat there barking until I reached him.

'Oh my god!' Helen and I gasped together. I knelt down gently to feel a pulse. There was none. I felt sick. I shook from head to toe and the tears could not be suppressed. The shock had done the same to Helen.

The body was Sylvia Miller's. Helen reached for the walkie-talkie and went straight through to Bill in his office at the station. While we waited, I looked down upon the torn and mutilated body of this sweet woman. It looked as though she had died of multiple stab wounds. Blood stains changed the colour of the branches and the tiny shrub leaves in this terrible confined space. The air stifled us both, smelling sharp and dank. Sylvia's clothes had been ripped, torn from her body and strewn on the surrounding area. No, this one could not be labelled a pristine murder. This was brutal, messy and cold-blooded. What in the world was happening? My eyes blurred with tears. My heart weighed heavy with anguish. I was so angry I needed to hit someone.

Helen and I pulled each other away from this ugly, hypnotic scene and gawped into space with the shock. It was only the sound of police cars, driving up the rough embankment that broke the trance. I saw Bill jump out of his car and run in, what appeared to be, slow motion towards us. He had plain clothes and uniformed officers with him. No protocol was adhered to when he threw his arms around the both of us. I felt cold, miserable and hurt. Helen and I wept some more.

Perhaps it had been a mistake to befriend Sylvia. Where does professionalism end and friendship begin? Helen, Maeve and I had talked earlier between ourselves of what an absolute brick the woman was. Bill led us slowly back to his car and took us home.

There must have been eight of us at our house. It was four forty-five. The sun had pretty well warmed our part of the world today yet ... I shivered. Bill had ordered the scene- of- crime officers out there along with everyone else that should be there. I was stunned to say the least. Perhaps because it was so unexpected. Jenko was beautiful. He never left my side. He nuzzled and licked and pawed to comfort me. I, in turn, snuggled up to his adorable face, petting his head, rubbing his ears. As for my man: it's a rare thing to spot any visible signs of fear on him. Mild anxieties yes, fear no.

I knew instinctively the turmoil he was in. His mind must have been like a washing machine. He imagined that the corpse could have been me.

I sipped coffee in silence and thought. I tried to ignore the team around me, muttering, striding around the room, gesticulating with flaying arms to make a point. Then I stood up.

'Bill do you know what I would like to do?'

'Go ahead sweetheart, tell me.'

'I'd like for Helen and me to take Jenks and pop over to the gym to work this off. Then we'll come back here, I'll take a shower and we'll share a light supper. What do you say? Sensible?'

'Sensible! Go for it! Whatever you have to do Marsha. Sounds good to me. You don't mind if I sign an extra minder on do you?'

'No of course not. Can we take Miguel?'

'The giant? I was hoping you'd suggest that. He's all yours. I'll meet you back here at, say, twelve thirty. Okay? I may have some of the guys with me. I'll let Hetta know. She's about the only person who'll enjoy this.'

I laughed. He was right. Hetta loved nothing more than ministering to us, our friends or our work colleagues - she loved it! Out would come the Cornish pasties, Danish pastries, and sandwiches. The men would never want to leave.

I grabbed my gym kit. We drove round to Helen's to find hers with Miguel in tow, a replica of the mythical Tarzan, and away to the gym.

Miguel came right in but parked himself with a newspaper. He wasn't reading it. His eyes were all over the place. We caught him laughing at us more than once as Helen and I put ourselves through some gruelling paces on treadmill, rower, cycling machine, weights and various other machines until we'd worked every inch of muscle on our bodies. A small hand towel had soaked up the sweat from my neck but my face was red and dripping. My fringe had sprung into curls again from all the moisture I'd generated. Miguel took a couple of sweaty bodies back to my place for showers, before we settled ourselves in the conservatory. Jenks followed before I could whistle him over. I knew that he wouldn't let me out of his sight.

For once, Bill showed up on time with his entourage. The feeling was one of lightness and confidence. These were professionals. We were all professionals. We must catch the killer. We must catch Ed Prescotte. Helen and I relaxed and discussed our feelings frankly. This was our own working strand of therapy, counselling, call it what you will. It worked for us. Bill left the two of us alone in the conservatory and took over the lounge with his men.

'You know Helen, I think the whole force likes to come to our house rather than the canteen. I used to think it was me with my magnetic personality, my warmth, grace and charm rather than Hetta's cooking. Now I'm more truthful with myself - I know it's Hetta's cooking!'

'Too right Marsha. Maeve's the same isn't she? And Mike and Kerri?'

That jolted me back to reality. Mike! What if Mike discovered the dirty dealings of his father? He spent most of his time over at our place but then again ...I thought, in my hazy memory of yesterday, that the kids said they might be "kipping" over at Mike's place tonight.

Weren't they booked for a show at Hull Theatre? Yes they were! I'd forgotten.

'Bill!' I blurted out my fears and cursed myself for being so busy I'd clean forgotten Kerri was even staying with us. 'Hell Bill how can I get a message to the kids to come back here without arousing suspicion?'

Now I really did freak out. If Prescotte couldn't get to me, he could threaten Kerri or harm her. Bill tossed the idea over to the group in the lounge.

'Calm down Marsha. A great deal can happen before the show tonight. We'll sort something out you'll see.' Helen chipped in.

'Like what Helen? Like what?' At that last outburst I heard the back door slam. The kids were back!

'Aunt Marsha are you there? What on earth is going on? You've got half the police station over here. Coffee morning is it?' sang the husky, rich voice of my incredibly beautiful niece. I couldn't help it but I grabbed hold of her and squeezed her so tight she couldn't catch her breath. Mike followed up behind her, fussing Jenks.

'What on earth's going on here Aunt Marsha? Are you having a party?' she half laughed looking puzzled.

Luckily Helen came to the rescue.

'Hello Kerri, Mike. The truth is that, unfortunately your aunt and I found a body this morning while we were out running Jenko. From the recent reports it appears that a killer is somewhere on the loose in Hull.'

That gave Bill the opening he needed.

'Yes you two. We were coming over to fetch you tonight after the show. You know what an old worry

140

worm your aunt Marsha is. Well for safety's sake we decided you must continue to stay here a while longer. We've reason to believe this psychopath is running loose in the city. That okay with you guys?'

'Great I love it here Uncle Bill!' Kerri shouted back at him, blowing him a kiss.

'Me too Bill, thanks. It's the food! I could live here forever.' Mike quipped licking his lips.

Thank you God, I whispered under my breath. 'Bill I wonder if you could get one of your men to go over and check my office. I won't be back in until tomorrow. Just to check that it's still locked up.'

'Will do love.'

With that, Bill dispatched the tall, slim, blonde P.C. Jonathan Milo to his destination and proceeded with his conference. This time he closed the lounge door, no doubt briefing his men on whose son was staying with us. I physically propelled the youngsters to the kitchen and ordered them to take their suppers upstairs. Considering the information that I held on Prescotte, I experienced another wave of panic.

'Helen. It's all well and good Kerri and Mike sleeping here but we know that Prescotte's on the run. He could easily meet the kids from college and take them off somewhere. Use them for ransom. Please don't tell me I'm paranoid.' I chided, throwing both my arms about.'

'Stop worrying Marsha. The same thought occurred to me too. I'll have a word with Bill. Yes, I'm sure an escort to and from college would ease our minds. We'll ask if that lovely P.C. Milo can go to college with them.

Didn't you say they only actually have to be in college three days a week for their course? The rest of the time they spend in the library?'

'That's right.That's what they tell me. As if - but could he keep a twenty-four-hour watch on them Helen? I know it's asking a lot but Kerri is like my own. If any...' Helen cut me off.

'Don't give it a second thought Marsha. It will be done. Just let Milo come back from checking out your office and we'll ask Bill to have words with him.'

I stretched my legs, rubbing the muscles in my thighs. I'd done a good workout and cleared my head. Dad pervaded my mind. He wouldn't shrink from this. Indeed, he wouldn't shrink from anything. I'd trudged this road before. I would protect the kids from Prescotte but I would not be afraid. I would not hide from Prescotte. I would go out and find him rather than wait for him to come to me. After having made my resolution, I talked it over with Helen. She joked about my so-called reputation from the heady action days in France, working on the case of a clever wedding deception. Yes, she said she would be with me all the way, as long as we applied common sense and took all necessary precautions.

As we had relaxed and talked, the telephone had been ringing non-stop. The incident room had apparently moved to my lounge. Bill came to join us briefly, mug in one hand, notebook in the other and pencil behind his ear. He closed the glass door behind him.

'Marsha,' he began. 'Got the first report on Sylvia Miller's body'...

'...Fire away Bill. I've my professional head on again now.'

'Well ... although Sylvia's body was an atrocious mess covered in stab wounds, she was dead before that occurred. Cause of death – bullet to the back of the head.' He read the expression on my face before he said more. 'You will both take those bulletproof vests from upstairs before you go anywhere. I'll fetch another one from the station for myself. In other words girls, he's armed. So must we be.'

'Gotcha Bill. Thanks.' He kissed me on the cheek, gave me a quick squeeze of the hand and joined the rest of them. I knew this was a preliminary meeting with his closest and brightest colleagues. Tomorrow they would be working in the field and from the station. Their little tete- a- tete's did not occur frequently but it was never a problem. Very occasionally I may have brought a female client back here if she was too afraid to speak openly in my office. We were an incredibly easy-going family network.

The warm wind had become cooler. I slipped a sweater on and wandered into the garden. Jenks and Helen followed, hot on my tail.

'Would you ever have dreamt that Eddie Prescotte, that lovely quiet man could turn into this obsessed monster Helen? It's so unbelievable.' Jenks was so close to my body that his huge tail as thick as boat rope beat on my leg. This was a reminder that he was still there.

'You know Marsha, it's going to be a terrible task when it's all over, telling Mike and Kerri.'

'Ain't that the truth friend.' I answered feeling so sad, fleetingly thinking of Mike's future. We could see from the opening of the fence, the patrol coming back. I knew exactly what P.C. Milo had to say before he said it.

My office had been ransacked but the locked files had not been tampered with. That being the main concern, although all of the important documents on this case were locked in the safe, upstairs in our bedroom. Not only that, Jenko slept in a large basket on the landing. Nothing would get past him. We ushered Milo into the conservatory. His face held steady yet his eyes spelt out a forlorn look.

'Don't worry P.C. Milo, about the office I mean. I half expected it. Now what's that your holding in that polythene bag?'

I looked closely as he described it and where he'd found it. I knew too well what it was. I'd seen it countless times before. It was two large chunks of a woollen sweater – Eddie Prescotte's old gardening sweater - found caught up between two new nails that I'd hammered into the wall only yesterday. (I needed to hang up large bulldog clips with my expenses and petrol receipts on. Well it wasn't a perfect job and they were exceedingly large nails.) 'Just as well' I said out loud, pleased with myself, 'I think the Inspector will be well pleased with your find young constable. Did you find anything else by the way?'

'Well, I don't think your husband will mind me telling you ma'am, but I called forensic in. There were some beautiful footprints left in there. I'm sure he must have been disturbed while he was on the job.'

'Oh he's disturbed all right!' I said wryly - couldn't resist it.

'Well the point I was making ma'am is this. The footprints are so good because his shoes were covered in mud on the soles, only there was a fine chalky powdery substance all around the actual shape of the shoe. I'm pretty sure our men will have a good idea where he's been hiding.'

'Well now that is excellent news Milo.' I breathed in a deep rejuvenating breath. 'I think perhaps you should relay that to your inspector don't you? Help yourself to a coffee on your way. Oh and tell him I said it was okay.'

He frowned back at me.

'I mean to help yourself to coffee.'

'Oh yes, and thank you ma'am.'

'My pleasure.' I said and let him get on. 'What do you make of that lot Helen?'

'I'll tell you what I think Marsha. We will catch him. I know we will.'

CHAPTER THIRTEEN

The next two weeks proved unbelievably uneventful. Helen and young Milo gave me a hand to put the office back together again; not too much damage done. My priority had been to order a new reinforced door. It must have taken amazing strength to get through my locks, bolts and safety chain. But then Prescotte was a fit strong man. He'd also left behind a large claw hammer and giant metal lever of some description, again confirming that the prowler had been disturbed in his deed. Jenks and I had just finished a bacon butty when the phone rang. I ran into my small kitchen area for kitchen roll to wipe my hands. I was a holy terror for answering the phone with greasy fingers. It was Kerri.

What she had to say unnerved me momentarily.

'I'm so sorry Kerri. No you can't. Bill's orders sweetheart. I'm delighted Mike's dad has been in touch. Where did he want to meet you? At the theatre? Sorry honey you won't be able to go back with him after the show. Well I know he's a big bloke and can take care of you (and how) but you know how protective Uncle Bill is. Anyway you only went to the theatre a couple of weeks ago. What's on? Oh right. Yes I love the Shakespeare Company too darling. Look, I'll tell you what. Why don't Helen and I double up, go with you both and bring you home as normal? Great.That's settled then. At least you'll get to see the performance, I'll enjoy it too and Uncle Bill will have one person less to worry about. Good girl. Come home for your tea as usual. Bring Mike and we'll go from here.'

I rang Bill immediately to relate the phone call and make sure he'd be home for tea at the same time as Kerri and Mike. We'd have a cheery informal chat about Shakespeare and throw in enquiries about Prescotte at the same time. He'd also have time to cover the grounds of the theatre inside and out with first class officers in plain clothes.

Teatime came around quickly. But then mealtimes never ever came fast enough for Jenks, Kerri, Mike or myself. The three of us were seated at the table when Bill arrived home at a respectable hour for once. We all shouted "hi" together as Bill took to the bathroom to wash his hands.

'Hi gang! Wow, this looks good. What are we celebrating?' He asked scanning the table Hetta had laid out with such loving care. Juicy chicken portions, French fries, onion rings and fresh garden peas sat in front of us all. In the middle of the table sat a blackcurrant jelly trifle, shortbread, jam roly-poly cake plus a handful of colourful marzipan cakes.

'Don't worry Bill, you haven't forgotten a birthday or an anniversary. We simply thought it would be fun to have a lovely tea together before we galloped off to the theatre.' I winked at Kerri and Mike, 'Didn't we guys?'

'Terrific! What's on then? Would I like it?' Bill feigned no knowledge of the evening's planned events.

'Uncle Bill. You don't like Shakespeare! You can't stand him! So I won't bother to tell you which play it is.'

'Aw, come on Kerri. Tell Uncle Bill.' Bill teased her, as always, without remorse

'I promise I will listen with the utmost patience.'

After a beguiling wink from "Uncle Bill," she relented.

'It's Hamlet. The Royal Shakespeare Company is over here doing it. It will be fantastic.'

'Okay babe. Whatever lights your candle.' That had the kids in stitches. We exchanged friendly banter during the meal. I deliberately left the wine off the table. I needed to stay sober in order to note the progression of the evening in minute detail. It was Bill who edged the conversation around to more important matters.

'Anyone heard from Bob - Mike, Kerri, Marsha?'

'Oh! Of course you don't know Bill do you?' Mike started quite innocently.

'What's that then young man?' Bill asked so naturally, pouring himself another cup of tea.

'Dad rang me Bill! He's okay! God we've been so worried about him haven't we Kerri? Said he'd been away for a night or two to think. He was still really upset about mum even though they were parted. He said he'd try and meet us at the theatre. He didn't mind that you and Marsha said we're to live here for a while. He said thank you by the way for looking after us while this madman's on the loose.'

'Oh think nothing of it young man. We enjoy having you. I'll let the station know later, to take your dad off the missing person's list, I mean. I'm pleased he's back and better.'

'Thanks Bill. He sounds much better. Can't wait to see him.'

'Me too son, me too.' Bill said without a flinch.

We kept our eyes on our food. A second or two of

148

eye contact would have blown the whole thing. Munching away and thoroughly enjoying every minute of it, in my mind I had a fictional bet with myself. We were now playing cat and mouse with Prescotte. He wouldn't show up. He would know immediately that the kids would tell us he'd been in touch. So what would he do? He would reckon that we'd have the theatre well covered but what about the house? What about the office again? No doubt Bill had thought of this too. He's always on the same wavelength anyway. I'd mention it later, upstairs, before we went. Helen had eaten at home to save herself ample time to shower and change for the evening out - just for this evening as Bill was around. Tomorrow morning, bright and very early, she was to move in to our home quite covertly.

The hour arrived and we intrepid theatregoers found ourselves in some good seats in the centre. Armed with my tiny binoculars, I knew that I would enjoy this play. Helen and I had decided how to use the binoculars discreetly and to our advantage.

Mike and Kerri had that excited look in their eyes as the play began. They even managed to hold hands at the same time as hanging on to their binoculars for a better view. Although I could see the entire theatre in front of me and to the side of me, there was no way I could see behind me. I relied upon other eyes to do that.

The first interval came and went. We were three quarters through this fine performance when I spied a familiar figure heading for the gents. I recognised some of the plain-clothes police who knew me quite well. The one whose eye I caught nodded to me. He went after our suspect to see if he could make out a positive identification. But it turned out to be a false alarm.

In my wisdom, I felt it more sensible to let the police take over all the observation work and allow myself the luxury of enjoying the play, despite feeling edgy. It was so good to visit the theatre.

Normally I would relax into a performance but my instincts held me on alert My palms were sweaty but then these places become like hothouses when they are full up and tonight was packed out. Well now, the end of the performance came without a hitch! Yes, a false alarm, set up by Prescotte himself. It had become a lethal game. Helen walked up the ramp to reach the exit with Kerri on one arm and Mike on the other. I dawdled listening to comments that others were making. It was pleasurable. I've never heard a bad word said yet of the Royal Shakespeare Company. It was a superb evening. The crowds were thick. I couldn't see the other three but I knew they would wait at the outside door for me. I felt a jostle in my side. Then I felt a sharpness, a pain in my side. I turned. His eyes glowered into mine.

'Just a taste Marsha. Do I have a treat in store for you.' I grabbed hold of him and head-butted him in my anger. Not particularly lady-like, I appreciate that, but needs must! Two of our men caught the scuffle immediately and raced down the aisles. They couldn't get through the density of four, five, six deep of the snail-paced gossiping theatregoers. Too late! He mingled quickly in the crowd. But I'd given him something to think about. Yes Eddie Prescotte, we'd have a day of reckoning you and I.

I made it to the outer door clutching my side. Helen saw at once the blood on my hand.

'Take the kids home Helen. Martins and Hill will run me to the hospital. See you back at the ranch.' I managed a cheeky grin in order that it might convey a reassurance to her, only her frown dispelled that illusion all too quickly. Kerri screamed when she saw the blood and my hand gripping my side.

'Go Helen - now! I'll be fine.' Helen knew better than to argue or debate on such matters. I was not in the throes of death. He didn't intend to kill me, oh no. I could feel the wound measured about eight inches long and it had a depth to it. He could have rammed the blade home if he'd had a mind to but he hadn't. He wanted to play the game and he wanted to win. Mike and Kerri never even saw him. Eddie Prescotte had really flipped over the top now. He could not be sane. The wildness in his eyes betrayed his murderous intent. That's all I can say: kind of defies description. The way things were going, I couldn't see us taking him alive.

CHAPTER FOURTEEN

I nursed my dressed wound, whilst mulling over recent events, under the hair dryer at my local hairdresser's. Helen sat at the back of the shop reading mags. My stylist, Charmaine, had commented that I had little to say which she found unusual. I feigned early pre-menopausal systems. That brought a chuckle. I loved having my hair done. It seemed to be the only time I really sat still and took stock of the situation. Bill, as you would imagine, had become manic in his protective role. He wanted me to have twenty-four-hour protection or go to the station with him everyday. It took me two days to calm him down. After all, a flesh wound with eight stitches was not critical. Now I had a theory. Prescotte had already killed Lockburn or rather I had surmised that he had. I could not be too sure just how many killings he was responsible for. I had visited the psychiatrist at Wakefield; the one attached to the force, to ask him for a psychological profile on this man.

That gave me a whole new hypothesis to work through. The fact that he could have a phase of pristine murders, then visit a victim for a second time and kill in a different manner made me wonder. That is, if he did kill Sylvia. At any rate, I didn't think it was really me that he was after. I thought it was a smoke screen. It diverted attention away from his real target - Bill. Bill had a shrewd mind and his deduction skills were pretty renowned now. He was a kind of modern day Sherlock. If anyone could find him and the evidence to put him away for life then Bill could. I was of no use to him. If he had killed me, Bill would have hunted him down to the ends of the earth if necessary. So at some time it would be Bill he would have to deal with, not me or any other members of the family.

It had become a great strain trying to appear normal with Mike around. He still had no idea it was his dad who'd attacked me. When eventually this case was solved, I had no idea how we would handle Mike. My latest theory was confined to secrecy. Only my brain knew about it.

Helen and I were to meet Maeve at her lodgings straight after my hair do. I would put the hypothesis to her.

Jenks acted like a fool when Maeve greeted us all at her door. She followed Jenk's act in exactly the same manner, speaking rather stupidly, of how he was her "lovey" and "oh what a handsome prince you are" followed by "my monster chocolate button".

'Honestly Maeve, this dog brings out a hidden persona in you!' I laughed hugging her and attempting to climb over Jenks' body to make some progress into the hallway. Everyone else appeared to be out. That's probably why Maeve asked me to go round at two o'clock.

'And how's my brave girl then? Didn't shake you up too much I hope. You poor thing.'

'Not at all Maeve. A bit sore, that's all.'

'And what about Bill? How's he handling all of this?' she asked, ushering Helen and I into the small sitting room.

'Oh you know Bill. Anything that hurts me, hurts him. He'll get over it. He's calmed down an awful lot. Doesn't stop him being paranoid every minute of every day though. It's poor old Helen here, I feel sorrow for, trailing around like a bloodhound.'

'Rubbish Marsha. Beats catching up on paperwork in the office.' She beamed, stroking Jenko's large head.

'This is nice Maeve.' I had picked up a bronze of the Buddha. 'I've been promising myself one of these for ages.'

She only half heard me though. She's so punctual she must have put the kettle on three minutes before I arrived. There she was wheeling in a pot of tea plus biscuits on a hostess trolley.

'Right let's settle down and tell me what it is that is so important.'

I told Maeve of my theory. I could see she was impressed by the way she started to shuffle around on the spot. I'd noticed this idiosyncrasy from one of our first meetings. When she is excited or animated, her legs take on a life of their own!

'But what if you're wrong Marsha?' she questioned, whilst offering me another fig biscuit.

'I don't think I am Maeve but of course I can't be absolutely positive and let's face it, who knows what goes on in the mind of a psychopath. Honestly, you should have seen his eyes. God only knows what's happened to twist him up like this.'

'Yes', said Maeve cautiously, 'and let's not forget what Lucy's neighbour said about him. It could be he's blamed himself for the alternative lifestyle Lucy adopted to boost her income. You know, the "Madonna/whore" thing that many men keep in their heads. They put their women on pedestals like untouchable queens, whilst in the next breath they want sex because they can't control their lusting bodies and go to prostitutes. And they think women are complicated.' We all laughed heartily.

Well,' I went on, 'supposing I execute my next plan in tune with my theory. That it's Bill who's the greatest threat to him being caught and put away. What about sending Kerri and Mike to my sister's place down south?'

'That's a good idea,' Maeve said in her ultra-discerning voice. 'But I think you should do that anyway Marsha. Things are livening up a wee bit aren't they?' Helen, nodded wisely.

'I wondered Maeve if you would like a drive down there? I was hoping to take them myself in the morning with Helen in tow of course.'

'Are you sure you're up to it? I can make myself free all day tomorrow. In fact, yes, it would do us good. I can relieve you and Helen with the driving too. How's that?'

'Can you drive my great old blue Volvo estate? We have to have large vehicles you see. It's the best way to cart Jenks around.'

'My dear girl, I can drive Landrovers and army tanks if I have to. We'll say no more about it. Will you ring the college?'

'Yes I'll do it when I go back. Have to ask Bill to let P.C. Milo resume his normal duties. Don't want him reporting the youngsters missing when I've got them with me!'

Our plans were set for the morning. I'd phoned college and explained. No problem. Both young students knew what they had to read and what essays to prepare.

155

I took phone numbers so that they could ring their personal tutors for help if and when they needed it. Bill felt much better as Helen, Maeve and Jenks would be on hand if my trip began to go pear-shaped! I could not envisage anything at all going wrong on a straightforward trip like this.

CHAPTER FIFTEEN

Okay, so how wrong can you be? It all began with Mike's distinct lack of boisterousness in the back of the car - it was unnerving and so unlike him. I kept glancing in the mirror as I drove. Kerri's face was bloodless. She was obviously worried about Mike. He looked as though he'd been crying, by the slight streaks down his face. I wondered if he'd heard something. We'd only been on the road for fifteen minutes. I had halted at the traffic lights on the A63, which seemed to change quickly from red to green. Yet in that small space of time, Mike had jumped out of the car and sped across an open field running adjacent to the road. Helen too jumped out and followed him. Kerri screamed! The dark blue Merc. behind me, charged right up the rear of my car. Great! Now what?

I pulled in to the car park close by me, followed by an irate driver shaking his fist and mouthing obscenities that I'd heard a thousand times before. I wound the window down and allowed him to call me everything from a pig to a donkey until he said he would be contacting his solicitor as well as his insurance company.

Before I had the chance to open my mouth to shout out the "Riot Act", Maeve tactfully "shoved her spoke in" and announced that she was my solicitor. Would he please address her and not me? She also made him understand, without a shadow of a doubt, that he was tailgating and it would cost him. She didn't give him the chance to say any more, having leaned across me and wound the window back up pretty quickly. The damage to our car was minimal. The bumper had changed shape that was all! Helen, although she had given immediate chase after Mike, had in fact lost him. So - with my minder back in the car, we headed out of the car park to cruise a while, looking for a place to stop for a drink and "cool off" somewhat.

Maeve spotted a small roadside café quite quickly. It would do. We needed to get out of the car, take in a change of scenery; anything to shake off our anger at the driver and Kerri's dramatics over Mike. Our faces were expressionless as we trouped into the café. I ordered coffee, sandwiches and scones and sat down. I lit a cigarette. (I shouldn't have done - I had secretly applauded myself for doing so well. Nevertheless - needs must. I lit up!) Helen looked down at the grubby ashtray on the table so I presumed we were sitting in a smoking zone. Looking nonchalantly away indicated that she would not judge me for my lapse in resolve. Maeve took the same stance. Dragging quite furiously on my cigarette, I launched a verbal attack at my niece.

'Right Kerri. What was all that about? Huh? Don't say you don't know. Your face soured like a wet week as soon as we set off.'

She burst into floods of tears, as you would expect. I relented slightly, gave her some hugs and wiped her beautiful glossy hair away from her face otherwise it would soon be matted together with the wet tears. Helen threw a glance that said "go easy Marsha..."

'Oh Aunt Marsha I'm sorry, I really am sorry. Mike and I were eavesdropping last night. We know the real reason for the wound in your side.'

Kerri's speech was now stifled with sobs. What could I chastise her for? Eavesdropping occupies so much of my time.

'Where's Mike going Kerri? Back to his father?' Helen asked gently.

'Yes,' she croaked unwillingly.

'Well I don't for one minute expect you to tell me where he is and he'll have moved now anyway.' I muttered more to myself than to her. 'What I am going to do is take you home to your mother. What's more, you are going to stay put until this is all over.'

I dismissed all her protestations and about-turned for my original destination: my sister's. Good old Maeve talked to Kerri in a kindly, yet seemingly pedantic manner that quietened her for the rest of the journey. Exhausted to the extreme, Kerri fell asleep and even snored in the back seat whilst we women chatted and planned our next move.

'... and Bill knows nothing of your theory on Prescotte Marsha? That you believe Prescotte wants to kill him - Bill I mean.' Maeve asked, running a brush through her brillo-pad-like hair.

'No. I don't want him to know anything about this. I'd rather lay my own contingency plans with you first. That's if your up for it Maeve.'

'Course old girl. There's a lot more to me than meets the eye. Or did you know that?'

Smiling through my anxieties, I zoomed down the M1 to my sister's, hoping against hope that Maeve, Helen and I could pull this off without any of us getting hurt.

'Well hello Nance!' I shouted, sailing through the door of the only listed building in the village. Nancy lived in an

159

old converted farmhouse at the East end of the village. Cost thousands to achieve the results I was staring at – this wonderful conversion. My sister and I had remained close despite living at opposite ends of the country. But what were a few hours drive on the motorway? We had become firm allies supporting one another when mother tried her hand at trying to mould us into her likeness. I had relayed our latest escapade over the phone. She knew that as soon as we had Prescotte behind bars, I would have kerri over to stay again. She appreciated through all this that I would never ever compromise Kerri's safety. What a sweetie she was. Nothing fazed her, only the thought of me being in personal danger. She never worried unduly but always reminded me to stay aware. Nancy made soothing talk and gave plenty of hugs to her daughter before sending her up for a soak in the bath. She made sandwiches for us all and ushered us into the conservatory.

'I don't need to stress the importance of keeping Kerri strictly indoors - you know within your sight twenty-four-hours a day Nancy, do I?' I said biting into a beef salad sandwich, slurping mayonnaise down my chin. Maeve performed much more elegantly, dabbing her mouth with a napkin every forty seconds.

Steve my brother-in-law was at work. He's an architect. He was also well versed in my daily antics and quite frankly loved me for it. Nevertheless, Kerri's protection was paramount. I deliberately didn't tell Nancy much about the case. The less she knew the better. Suffice to know that Kerri must be protected until we had solved the case. I watched her body give a slight tremble or shiver as she stared out into the woodlands.

'Not good Nance, none of it. Try not to worry about

things.'

'It's you and Bill I worry about Marsha.' She flicked her shiny, newly rinsed auburn hair until the sun caught it. She was a beauty my sister. Kerri had inherited her slender figure and long legs. No I hadn't an envious bone in my body for sis. She laughed at me.

'You're crazy, Marsha. I'll bet Bill's told you a thousand times. With your brain, girl you could have done anything. But then again...'she sighed,'...you are your father's daughter.'

'I am, aren't I Nancy? I'm dad through and through. Do you mind?'

'God no love. I'm full of admiration for you. Just...be extra careful on this one.'

'Don't worry. Always am. Hey look at Jenks. He's emptied that bowl of water in seconds. 'Course, most of it's on the floor! I'll get him some more.'

'Sit still Marsha, I'll sort him. He's eaten his snacks too. I'll fill his feed bowl up again.'

What was it with Jenks? Wherever I take him, people treat him like a respected warrior, a prince of battle. Always feeding him, watering him, exercising him like a war-horse. My sister loved him. In fact she'd never seen anything like him. Who in the world has? We talked for an hour. Nancy left us only the once. She made sure Kerri went straight to bed to rest up. Convinced that Kerri would sleep for some hours yet, we all thanked Nancy for her hospitality and strode out to the nearby woodlands for a leg-stretch and made sure Jenko had a good run. Naturally he romped way ahead of us.

'Do you think Prescotte would take the trouble to try and get to Kerri, Maeve, Helen?' I asked my friends, assuming the possibility was a real one.

'Doubtful Marsha. He's on the run now.' Helen said with confidence.

'Well, he knows that if he's caught he'll be inside for life, though it's Mike I'm worried about.' Maeve chipped in.

'Me too.' I said soberly, encouraging Maeve to offer a little more input.

'No, I can't see Bob coming out here. What would he gain? And think Marsha. If you're right, he'll be concocting a plan targeting Bill, no one else. Bill knows nothing of this I take it?'

'Lord no Maeve. He's gone all "namby pamby" on my protection already. Thought he'd put me on twenty-four-hour guard with officers shadowing my every move. I told him I could not possibly work in that manner. It would scare all my clients and prospective clients right away. Said I'd settle for Helen.' I beamed across at said partner, who reciprocated with a deliberate idiotic smile.

'Of course - I must admit I have to say that I enjoy working with you Marsha, if that's the correct term.' I could see that Maeve dearly wanted to compliment me on my work but wasn't sure how to approach me.

'I think you know what I mean when I say that the actual spontaneity of your day has to be a good thing. You never know what you going to be doing next. My work is so factual, sometimes so boring too, even when I'm defending in court. I don't have the job satisfaction that you do. I suppose the grass always looks greener on the other side,' she murmured as we sauntered along the edge of the woodlands.

It was two thirty on an exceptionally glorious afternoon. We said our fond goodbyes and after warning one another of the obvious dangers we all faced, Maeve, Helen, Jenks and I set off for home, praying that Kerri would be safe with her parents. It was one less person for me to worry about.

Maeve was staying on with us until this case was finally mopped up. As a senior partner in a highly reputable law firm, she rang her counterparts on her mobile on the journey home. Of course they were intrigued and did not want her to return home, as she was so involved in the crime of the century as they saw it. They were admirably apologetic for my being injured but think of the extra business that it would bring their firm! Neither Maeve nor I batted an eyelid. Facts were facts. Life went on. That was the grim state of affairs. We were all used to it, realising only too well that the world does not stop revolving because bad things happen. So what now?

Almost home we called in at Alfie's for one of his excellent cappuccino coffees. I talked Maeve into trying one and wondered why I was surprised that she was not disappointed! Helen lapped hers up but then she loved them anyway. I rang Bill from my mobile to let him know that we were back. We would call at the office to pick up my mail and head straight back home after our long drive. I also rang Hetta to tell her that Maeve would stay a few more days. Could she prepare our meals accordingly? From Hetta's point of view, it meant more showing-off, of her culinary skills. From Maeve's point of view, good food would be a bonus towards the adventure she'd become embroiled in. From Helen's point of view, it meant keeping away from the Police Canteen. I stuffed the mobile into my already overflowing, exceedingly untidy, handbag-cum-holdall when Alfie appeared with the coffees.

'Hi beautiful.' He said planting a kiss upon my sweaty forehead. He shook hands with Maeve not risking a kiss in case she bit his head off. Instead of prancing off back to the counter he sat down and pulled up his chair between Helen and myself.

'This is in confidence of course, Marsha my dear,' he half whispered sounding for all the world like a modern-day Fagan. 'Remember when you once brought that lovely niece of yours in 'ere with that boyfriend of 'ers, my lovely?'

I nodded expectantly.

'Well 'e was in 'ere about an hour ago. In a right state 'e was. Ordered a bacon sarny and a coffee. Hadn't quite enough money so I told 'im not to worry. I fed 'im, then 'e scarpered.'

'Thanks Alfie. Can I ask you a stupid question?'

'You can sweet'eart, but no I don't know where he went. I didn't ask an''e didn't volunteer any information. Is any of this info useful to you ducks?'

'Very! Thanks Alfie.' I placed a kiss onto his baldpate just to show him I appreciated him. He nodded, winked then moved away to carry on with his business of serving, shouting orders at his staff, before disappearing out of his back door for a crafty cigarette. Maeve's jaw dropped and her eyes rolled as if to jump headlong out of their sockets. No words were needed to speak of the anguish we both felt for the boy. We drank our fill of cappuccinos and called round to my office.

'Well it looks all right from the outside Marsha,' Maeve observed. 'No broken windows, no forced entry.'

Helen surveyed the area before she'd let us enter the premises.

'So far, so good Maeve. Come on Jenks. You first,' I said as I unlocked the door with the care and precision of dealing with an unexploded bomb. Jenks had a good old sniff around the reception area before coming back to me.

'Good boy Jenks. Come on then. Good God, look at the pile of mail Maeve. Sure you wouldn't like to join up with me and leave that boring old solicitor's practice?' I sniggered with a half-cocked eyebrow.

'Helen would you like a break. No, don't look like that. I'm perfectly all right with Maeve and Jenks in my own office. What about checking in at the Station and giving Bill an update.'

I did not really want Helen to leave but I thought she could use a breather. I'd much sooner have her around when her brains were fresh.

'Thanks Marsha I'll do that. I'll call at my place and pick up some more white shirts too. Is there anything we need, that I can pick up in town while I'm about?'

'No thanks Helen. If you get back to us say, in a couple of hours? That okay with you?'

'Absolutely fine. Sure you'll be...'

'Go Helen, before I change my mind. Tell Bill these are my instructions.'

Helen laughed, 'Oh don't worry yourself on that score. You know what he's going to say the minute he sees me! "Why aren't you with my wife?"'

I practically pushed her out of the door, begging her to make the most of her freedom for the short time she had.

Maeve and I scooped up the mail. I halved it so that I could share the workload, thereby getting finished much more quickly. We compared notes as we went along.

'A cheque here Marsha, for, two hundred and twenty-five pounds. Nice one! Moreover, a nice thank you note. Well done! Request for appointments, ditto, ditto' on she went, tearing open one envelope after another.

'Oh look at this one Maeve, this is a lovely thank you. I found a missing teenager, young girl. I got lucky with her. Only missing ten days, trail still hot. That was easy but you have to admit that, taking a young mixed up girl back to her weeping parents, is job satisfaction for you. Hey and look at this one, that's a photo of a kitten Bill rescued from up a tree. Isn't that sweet? Belonged to a child of eight. I wish all my work gave me such a good feeling...

'...Well, well, well.' I said, reading a grubby piece of paper I'd ripped out of a dirty, used, brown envelope. It's from Mike, Maeve.' As I unfolded it, she moved across to stand behind me and peered over my shoulder. I read it out aloud to make doubly sure we both understood it.

I'm with my dad. You're not going to catch him because I'm going to help him. Stay away from us both. Tell Kerri she'll never see me again.   Mike

So why did I express no surprise? It didn't matter that Ed was a guilty man. He was Mike's dad. His mother was dead - this was all he had.

'Isn't it sad Marsha?' Maeve said, trying to brush away a tear as though it was an unwanted spec of dust.

'Oh yes Maeve. Sad it is. But it doesn't alter the fact that Ed has to be caught, has to stand trial and if convicted will go down for life. Then what will Mike do? Do you suppose they'll try to leave the country? Is that what the reference to Kerri means?'

'No. I think Prescotte's put him up to it to throw us off the scent a while. No Marsha, I hate to say it but I think your theory is right. I think he will try to leave the country, but not until he's got rid of the one man who can put him away.'

'Bill.' I sighed with a heavy heart.

CHAPTER SIXTEEN

Helen never had the chance to come back to me. Her mother had been taken into hospital with a suspected heart attack so Helen had taken compassionate leave. She asked if she should keep in touch by phone. I told her in no uncertain manner that, no that would not be all right! I should be the last person in the world she must concern herself with at a time like this.

So some of my anxieties and frustrations would be taken out on the garden. It had become so neglected, that I'd given myself a full day off to sort it out. The weeds stood taller than the dahlias and crysanths! I'd mown the lawn, cut the hedge, and had achieved three quarters weeding of the flowerbeds. It would take me another half-hour and I could sit down for a break in my now-restored, beautiful garden. It was a real pain to have to work in this heat but there was no alternative. This was my allotted day for the garden so I psyched my self up to get on with the job. Even Jenks had the sense to sit in the cool passageway. His jaws were dropped open and his jowls jiggled about whilst he panted. It made him look as though he was laughing at me. His ears missed nothing though. The gate clanged! Jenks was up and away!

'Can't you relax for a minute woman?' the voice shouted, as she strode up the path with Jenks bouncing at her heels.

'Sally! My God! Why didn't you ring girl?' I screamed, scaring Jenks half to death. He jumped forward right into Sally's path. It was inevitable Sally could not defy the fall she was heading for, straight into the giant pink Hydrangea. Well that was it. In she went, head first, followed by Jenks who thought it was a fantastic game. I needn't have worried. She came up laughing. The gate fastener clanged again. It was Maeve back from a shopping trip. Jenks ran back and forth not knowing which playmate to go for first. Maeve and I each offered an arm to pull Sally into an upright position.

'I think this calls for G and T's all round. Come on girls. We'll go for introductions when we've got Sal sorted out. I discreetly shut the back door so that Jenks couldn't perform any more tricks. I was thankful to get in from the heat and into the lounge where two fans were competing with each other to see which could create the most draught.

'So... what brings you to our neck of the woods Sally? It's fantastic to see you. It really is. Maeve here, is staying with us while we resolve an extremely important case. I don't know if you're aware of it over in Liverpool but...'

'...The Pristine Murders Marsha. That's why I'm here.'

'Oh?' Maeve and I stared in fascination.

'Yes I know all about it girls. 'Course I would wouldn't I. When I told my boss it was my best friends who were handling the case, he briefed me on all the info he had and told me to get over here. Now don't look like that Marsha,' she said, watching my eyebrows rise and my lips tighten.

'Same procedure as before. If I help you guys out, can you clear it for me to have first crack at the story.'

'You can for me Sal and I'm sure Bill will get permission to O K it. They cleared you last time and we heard you received a commendation for the way you handled the story. I can't see any problems.

Why? What do you have? What do you know that we don't?'

'Well I thought we'd compare notes. I have loads of info.' She fired off with a gut load of enthusiasm.

Sally had accumulated much of the same information as we had but for one salient point. She had documents to say that Prescotte had in fact been admitted to a mental institution at the beginning of his marriage. It was at the time that Mike was still a baby, some eighteen months old. Lucy visited her G.P. as she had watched Eddie's problem developing; an obsessive and compulsive disorder that frightened and depressed her. Both of them were subjected to treatment. Lucy's depression was brought under control with good medication and a professional ear to bend. She also had the child to care for which in turn, gave her the resolve to get well. Ed's obsession took the form of extreme cleanliness, particularly in the kitchen. The kitchen equipment not only had to be clean but glassware and metal had to shine. He drove her half-crazy cleaning and shining chrome fittings, the kettle with matching milk jug and sugar basin. The windows had to be cleaned everyday. Lucy came to a standstill not only from the sheer physical exhaustion but also from the mental anguish of knowing that every morning she rose out of bed, the ritual cleaning would begin again.

He used a toothbrush for cleaning tap fittings and then polished them off with a duster. As if that wasn't bad enough, he began to sharpen, clean and polish the kitchen knives. Sally read out loudly a transcript of a conversation between the psychiatrist and Prescotte,

Dr. Soames: *Mr Prescotte, why do you think you spend so much time cleaning and polishing glassware and metals to the extent that this equipment is without blemish? Surely it must be extremely difficult to retain this condition of scrupulous cleanliness in a kitchen. After all that is where so much of the daily household tasks takes place.*

Prescotte: *I have to do it! Must be clean at all times! The knives are so beautiful. Their shape, their absolute loveliness. Formed by the gods. Mustn't be tainted.*

Dr Soames: *Why mustn't they be tainted? A kitchen is for working in. For preparing food in. Normal cleaning and care of food preparation is all that is called for. If all of our home environment was in such a continued pristine condition then we would never have the day to day germs coming into contact with our bodies; thereby never building up a natural immunity in our systems.*

Prescotte: *... But it's not us men doctor. Don't you see? It's the women. They don't know how to clean and they can't keep themselves clean.*

Dr: *Can you explain further, explain exactly what you mean Mr Prescotte? Are you saying that womankind is in some way dirty and that man is not? That's rather a distorted view of the opposite sex don't you think?*

Dr.'s note:	*Prescotte's eyes become wild as he's trying to work out what to say. His breathing is laboured. His body is sweating and he is clenching and unclenching his fists.*
Prescotte:	*Women are filth doctor. They have to be cleansed. Not like us.*
Dr:	*Are you saying that all women are filth or just certain women?*
Prescotte:	*Prostitutes, they're dirty.*
Dr:	*Have you visited prostitutes for sex then?*
Prescotte:	*Course I have. All men do don't they. That's what they're there for.*
Dr:	*But why do you go for sexual gratification to women you think are dirty? Aren't you afraid of catching some morbid disease from them?*
Prescotte:	*Not me Doc. I scrub myself everytime I've been with one.*
Dr:	*If you hold this view about women, then why did you get married?*
Prescotte:	*Well I wanted a child didn't I? They've got the magic. They can bring kids into the world. That's all I wanted a son. I got what I wanted. No use for the woman now...*

'Need I go on or would you like me to let you read the rest of this stuff later?' Sally asked indulgently.

'No thanks Sal, I think we all get the gist of that. Pity we didn't know about this sooner. Tell me, is this psychiatrist still around and practising?'

She immediately pulled out the name and address of a private clinic in Bridlington, headed by the doctor's name Ronald Jaylor-Soames.

'Looks like our next port of call. What do you say girls?' Our party all nodded in agreement. 'Right we're on! I'll clear it with Bill. Sally can you set up an interview for us? If all four of us go down we have safety in numbers. What do you say?'

Sally beamed with a mischievous look in her eye. That told me she'd already set it up.

'Well? What time and what day Sal?'

'Tomorrow twelve thirty - only an hour's drive. Now how about another G and T for your old buddy Marsha?'

Once proper introductions were over, we re-arranged the bedrooms so that Maeve took the box room. The Lord only knew what Bill would say at teatime.

We waited until six thirty and then I put a call through to ask what time Bill would be home. He'd left at five o'clock. It took between ten and fifteen minutes depending on traffic for Bill to arrive home. So where was he? I panicked at first. Luckily, the girls calmed me down. As they so logically put it, Bill could be anywhere. He could have called in at Alfie's, at the flower shop as he knew I loved to have flowers in the house at all times, or at the barbers. In fact there could be any number of reasons why he might have detoured. Yes my mind said but Bill always rang me when he set off for home, as he often was sidetracked. I tried his mobile. It was switched off. Not a good sign.

He purposely left it switched on at all times because of the situation we were in, in order to keep communications open. I could see the anxiety begin to creep up on Maeve's face.

We waited until seven o'clock and then allowed Hetta to serve our dinner. Although we ate, no one ate with gusto. I rang the station again as I trawled my trembling fingers through my hair, to ask if he had to call somewhere on his way home. No he hadn't. Now they were concerned. I wasn't quite sure what to think. We sat in mutual silence and by the furrowed brows I glanced at around me, everyone was thinking and thinking hard. Ten fifteen and still we sat. Then the shrill of the phone startled us all into jumping up at the same time to grab the hand piece. I got there first. It was the station.

Bill had last been seen, climbing into a police panda car. This car had been found on wasteland some five miles away and it had been torched. Bill was nowhere to be seen.

CHAPTER SEVENTEEN

Superintendent Philips called us into the station. He didn't mind in the least that three of us had crammed ourselves into his tiny office.

'Marsha, I'm extremely sorry, but as yet there is absolutely nothing I can tell you. Every officer out on the street, in their cars or on the beat, is keeping an eye out for Bill. I wondered' he paused for a second, 'I wondered if you might have an idea, any idea at all where he might have headed off to. On the other hand, if indeed he's had scent of Prescotte and is off on his own?'

My heart had sunk to my shoes, 'Sorry - I was hoping against hope *you* might know something.'

Despondency took a hold of us all.

'The only thing I can think of,' I started my brain working overtime,' is that Bill would probably think the same as us. Prescotte is either hiding out near a port waiting to catch a boat or he's at an airfield. I think he'll try and kill Bill before he escapes abroad.' There I'd said it.

'But surely you don't think he'd do anything while he's got the boy, Marsha?' The chief sounded so sure. I wish I'd felt the same.

'Wait a minute.' I said. 'What about this scenario then? In his warped mind, Prescotte may want to visit the place that Lucy finished up at, in order to prove something to himself. If he goes to that flat that she rented, where she practised her prostitution, it may give him the final verification that he needs - you know, that it was right and just to kill her. Why don't you ring Liverpool Police station? Ask them to send a detective round in casual clothes and give that neighbour a knock: the one Maeve and I spoke to and ask if there has been any sound of movement next door. Of course it could be kids or tramps or druggies but then again ... that's the best I can come up with chief. What do you say girls?'

'We've no leads at all at present. I say give it a go.' Maeve said turning to the rest of us one by one for affirmation.

'Right girls, would you all like to help yourselves to coffees in the canteen? I'll come and join you as soon as I have anything. I'll tell them it's a top priority, so we should have something within the half-hour. Shouldn't take them too long to get a couple of CID blokes out there to have a look around.'

We shuffled our feet, irritably, somewhat as though we were waiting for something else to happen. Slowly we managed to work our way across to the canteen. The officers already in the canteen seemed to share our despondency. No cheeky quips were forthcoming as they normally did. Just a nod and a wink in mutual worry came across. Sally went for sandwiches. Maeve flumped down first, cupping her chin in her hands. We others bleakly followed suit. Sally came back almost immediately having no queue to wade through. Well, there we all were looking for all our worth like we'd won and lost the lottery. Even Jenks couldn't pretend to wag and be happy.

'I really don't know what to think any more Maeve,' I moaned at her, feeling immensely sorry for myself.

'Marsha isn't it at times like this that your famous

176

intuition kicks in dearie?'

I reached for my glass of milk, sipping and staring idly up at the ceiling.'

'Yeah, you're right Maeve it is, only it's not working today. I've never felt so utterly useless in my life.'

Sally nudged herself into talking mode next.

'Oh come on Marsha. You are not thinking. Come on girl, engage your brain. Snap out of this apathy for God's sake.' Sally's nerves were getting the better of her.

'Now come on Sally, we're all so terribly worried we're going to go to pieces if we're not careful. That will do Bill no good whatsoever. Agreed?'

'Agreed.' We mumbled one after the other.

'Trouble is,' I said, more as an afterthought, 'I know what Sally is saying. I've been in some tough scrapes but something extra slams into my brain. I seem to know instinctively what will come next but here I'm so frightened because I'm floundering. This is Bill's life that's on the line girls.'

'Okay,' Maeve chipped in. 'Let's just sit down quietly and try and get into the mind of a psychopath.'

Now we all looked up and tried to assume an intelligent stature! That brought us all to book.

Maeve took our attention.

'Okay, here's what we have. Prescotte is much deranged. He'll also be on a "high" and it's a pretty sure bet he's got Bill with him. He's a compulsive-obsessive character, who we now know is extremely dangerous. Now I would not for one moment dismiss your theory

177

Marsha, when you imagine he may have gone back to the scene of Lucy's prostitution days but I, personally don't think so. He is angry with you and Bill for being so damned clever.'

She paused for a moment or two to gauge reaction before she went on.

'I think we should sit it out for half an hour until we know what's what in Liverpool and allow Marsha to sit a while and see if the good old magic ingredient kicks into her brain. We'll finish our milk and take a trot around the station's grounds with Jenko, see if we can toss some more ideas around.'

We ambled along together, heads down, looking more or less funeral bound. If only I had a clue, one small clue I could follow up. A positive lead. My thoughts escaped me.

'I wonder if there's a message on the answerphone in my office?' Their faces were dull, downcast. 'Now come on girls, I don't want either of you to pass out with enthusiasm. What do you think Jenks? Office?' Jenks was all for it. He knew the word and he knew the office. I would have to go now or he would never stand still. He twirled and frolicked like a toddler waiting to go to the fair.

'Well I can't think of anywhere else we should go to Marsha.' Sally chipped in. It would help to pass the time I suppose. What do you say, Maeve?'

'I'm game.' Maeve said in her deep, guttural voice.

'Right, we'll just pop back inside the station. Check on the progress.' I said, more positive than I'd sounded all day.

'No need Marsha.' Sally said as she pointed at the chief plodding across the grassed area.

'Sorry Marsha, no luck yet. Two of the Liverpool people are out there. They've checked with the neighbour and the other flat itself. Nobody's been near the place. But don't you worry. Our Bill's a wily character. I know he can take care of himself love. What do you propose to do now?'

'Go over back to my office and check the answer machine Chief. You never know. And it is considerably better than doing nothing at all.'

'Why not. But you must stay in touch. Any hunch, anything at all, you don't move without me. Understand. We don't want anything to happen to you too. Now do we?' He stated with authority, wagging his long thin, nicotined finger in my direction.

'Gotcha chief. I promise.'

'Good off you go and take it easy Marsha.'

Six minutes drive and we were back at the office. Somehow it looked clean and bright from the outside. I wonder why I'd never noticed it before. Probably because at this moment I could think of nothing else. I could see nothing else even in my mind's eye. So perhaps this is the first time I'd taken a good look at my little office. Yes I liked it. I like it a great deal. My name was up there. Dad would have been so proud.

We trooped in like a load of girl guides awaiting instruction. As soon as we entered I heard the bleep, bleep of the answer-machine. We eyeballed one another yet again, as if we were embarking on something mysterious, like ghostbusting! Maeve picked up the letters.

'Better open them Maeve. You never know.'

'Right you are.' Maeve complied without a second glance. I played back the recorder and we all instinctively crowded around to see if it would reveal a vital clue. We were all silently praying for Prescotte to make contact; any sort of contact. Just something. We were not at all disappointed!

Colour floods to the spot, dull purple.

The rest of the body is all washed out,

The colour of pearl.

In a pit of rock

The sea sucks obsessively,

One hollow the whole sea's pivot

The size of a fly,

The doom mark

Crawls down the wall

The heart shuts,

The sea slides back.

The mirrors are sheeted.

Then the voice:

180

Why hello there, clever Marsha Riordan. Remember your poetry. Remember all the literature you've taught. Ha! Ha! Ha! Great this isn't it! Come on now use your brains if you want to find old Bill before he comes to a sticky end! Ha! Ha! Well if you can't read this clue, well here's another one. Mrs Ramsey made some stockings to take to a little boy at the... Do you remember? Oh I rather think I've given part of the game away don't you Marsha. Because it is a game isn't it. I don't want anything to happen to old Bill until you get here old thing. Ha! Ha! Ha!

Then another voice broke through, a terrified voice.

Marsha don't listen to him. Bill is okay, so far. Dad is crazy. Please help us. Don't let him trap you Marsha...

The phone fell dead. I knew the second voice was Mike's. He was a terrified young man and by now, well aware of his father's madness.

'Well what was all that garbage about Marsha?' Helen asked, genuinely puzzled.

'I think I know. We're talking poetry and prose here. I'll have to play them back a few times to remember. Let's sit down girls. Helen can you take this down in shorthand for me and then write it up afterwards.'

'Yes but after we've run it through a few times you'll perhaps know these works anyway.'

We played it through five times. Helen scribbled up her ciphers and wrote it up in English.

'Get on to the chief Helen and give him this lot while I think.'

I lit another cigarette. The number I was smoking today far exceeded any thing like I'd smoked over the last month. Yes I knew where Mrs Ramsey took her knitted stockings to, very well. It was to the lighthouse, the very same name of Virginia Wolf's famous work. The other, the poetry, was a poem from a collection of Sylvia Plath. But, I couldn't put my finger on it. Yet, I didn't think it too important to know which one it was, I would look it up later. For now it was enough to have an image of Bill plunging over the cliffs somewhere near a lighthouse. Then it came to me.

'Eureka! Flamborough Head: The Lighthouse. He's got Bill holed up somewhere near the lighthouse, probably down below in the caves.'

'Yes!' My friends exclaimed together.

'You're a damn genius Marsha,' Maeve said, patting me on the back as if I was a star pupil at some academy.

'I'm not waiting for the boys in blue.' I stated with much authority. 'I'd better tell the chief that. In fact I ought to ask him to keep an extremely low profile with his men. If Prescotte sees a load of flashing lights and boys in blue, who knows what he'll do. No, we'll take off now. Jenks'll get Bill out of this mess. I know he will.'

CHAPTER EIGHTEEN

The adrenaline was up and working. I felt a rush of excitement mingled with fear as I set off with all my friends and Jenks in Bill's battered, blue Volvo estate car. Jenks was bright and alert. In all likelihood, he looked forward to a fishing trip! That's the only time he goes in this car - when Bill has a whim for fishing. However, should I be forced into a slushy sandy beach race – this is the car to do it in precisely because of its dilapidated condition.

It would not take long for us to reach Flamborough from our base in Hull. Piling along the A165, my head reeled with possible scenarios of what was happening to Bill. My imagination is so fertile I must have had poor old Bill dead and buried at least four times. I even imagined myself looking at his body on a mortuary slab. Maeve brought me down to the earth, almost as if she had read my thoughts.

'I wouldn't worry too much about Bill Marsha. He can take care of himself you know.'

'Only to an extent Maeve. Faced with a madman it's difficult for anyone. I only hope he's managed to talk to him, you know play the waiting game with him and what about Mike? God knows what this is doing to him.'

'No good speculating Marsha. Let's hope your hunch is right at least; that they are all at Flamborough Head.'

Well, here we were, standing upon a craggy cliff edge watching the water crashing into rocks below.

We had followed a dark winding road that led from the old lighthouse to the new one. The wind, which was mild in land, was actually blowing so strongly it was next to ferocious. I looked up at the moonlit sky only to see dark grey clouds chasing across it. The vision turned the moon into a jumping, fleeing, white ball desperate to be seen. To the west, the sky had already turned black. It was difficult to make out the difference between storm clouds and the night sky. The heavens appeared to me like a thick, merging mass. Worst of all it was coming our way. Maeve had had a hunch about the weather and made sure we all had our boots, scarves, gloves, raincoats and any other clothing item she could think of that would help shield us from the elements. I made sure we had two-way radios this time. Mobile phones would be useless. Where to look? Where on earth would we start? More to the point, what if I had completely misread the clever words of a maniac?

I let Jenks loose. With his intelligence and brawn, nothing would trouble him only a bullet from a gun. We split up and began the trudge along the cliff edge peering over the top of it at intervals. We couldn't see the point of climbing down the slippery slopes to the water's edge unless we had concrete reasons to do so. Maeve and Sally led the way. I followed with Jenks.

'Rum job! Eh Marsha?' Sally shouted to me against the ghostly, howling of the wind.

'I'll say Sal. Poor old Bill! He must be freezing out here. That's if he is here. Sally what about the tides too?'

'I've told you to stop worrying about Bill, Marsha.

We can't change what's happened. We have to deal with the immediate "here and now." Sally spoke with an urgency supposed to stem my anxiety. I suppose she thought it might help. Sympathy certainly wouldn't!

I jogged a little to keep up with Jenks. Sally and Maeve each had a pair of binoculars hung around their necks for what good they'd do in the moonlight. We'd arranged ourselves so that we would not be out of one another's sight for more than fifteen minutes at a time. Even so, fifteen minutes stalking in a head wind seemed at best like an hour. We had executed our routine twice by now.

The gods must have heard my complaints because the wind dropped. It was as though the lull had come by command. I was about to rejoin Maeve and Sally when I heard someone shout. It was muffled and barely audible, as you'd imagine against a screeching gale. We scuttled off to our meeting point. Both Maeve and Sally looked excited. Sally's eyes shone and sparkled as she batted her arms on her sides to gain more warmth. Maeve was so huddled up with a great woollen duffel coat complete with scarf around her face that it was impossible to even hazard a guess at what she was thinking. Her eyes were almost closed set against the wind too.

'We think we've seen something Marsha. Come on.' Garbled words gushed from Sally's mouth. I could hardly make them out. Maeve and I simply allowed ourselves to be pulled and guided in the appropriate direction. It must have been five hundred feet up a track adjacent to the cliff edge. Using the binoculars Sally told me where to look. Luckily, the moon's struggle for freedom from the clouds paid off.

185

It gave enough intermittent light to be of use. I focussed with careful directions from my good friend. I aimed for the rough waters where a 'V' shaped piece of rock jutted out. It appeared to be beside the entrance to a cave. I passed the binoculars back to Sally. Yes we all agreed it was a body.

I made no visible sign of emotion. I felt that all of my insides had caved in and landed in the pit of my stomach encouraging me to be physically sick. Maeve pulled me up sternly.

'Marsha get a grip! We have no idea who it is and we won't ever know unless we trek down there ourselves.' We all made to move when I halted the singular marchers.

'Hang on a minute girls. Supposing this is a trap. Supposing that's Mike down there being made to bait us. What good will it do, if this is a trap and we all end up hostages with no one to call for help? Sally you wait up here with Maeve.' She opened her mouth and swung her arms around in frustration,

'No I must insist you stay up here Sally. You and Maeve have a radio. I have the other. Here, take the car keys and the other torch. If I run into problems you'll see from up here. You can call for help and run. It's no good arguing about it. It won't do for us all to end up dead.'

I didn't stay around to listen to any more argument. I whistled Jenks over to my side and began edging my way down the old disused stairway. It was not a long journey down to the waterside. I looked up at the two statues, Maeve and Sally, their bodies positioned rigidly like Roman centurions. Their long coats flapped and blew around their legs, covering and clinging as though they'd been in contact with static. I glimpsed the body with my torch. It didn't need a close identification. I could see clearly that it was Mike. My throat dried up. I looked upwards towards my friends. They nodded. It looked as though they were about to follow me down until I radioed up,

'Hold on Sal, he could merely be unconscious – not....' I approached him stealthily, looking in every direction. The wind blew a curtain of hair across my eyes. A spray of freezing cold water caught the back of my coat but it did not seep into my other clothes. I bent down and touched the body gently.

'Mike. Mike can you hear me, it's Marsha?' I reached up to try to find a pulse in his neck.

Yes! There it was, in his throat, beating like the soft patting of a bongo drum. I shouted up to the others that it was Mike and that he was alive. I then pulled out the small revolver that I kept in my handbag and radioed back again!

'Right Sally, can you put a call through for help now? Ring the Coastguard. He'll contact Air and Sea Rescue at RAF Leconfield. Send Maeve down. We can hardly ring for ambulances and police cars, risking the atmosphere being filled with nothing but sirens, can we? You two can go with Mike to the hospital and come back for me. Agreed?'

Sally's voice said "yes" but I knew her heart shouted "no". All the same, she was handling the situation well. Her bravery has never been brought into question. Maeve climbed down slowly, cautiously never stumbling. Then all at once we were together, staring down at the cold, barely moving body of young Mike.

187

He had opened his eyes briefly and moved his hand as if to tell us to go. Maeve and I wrapped him up as best we could in two battered tartan blankets. He must have been suffering from hypothermia at least as well as nursing a nasty wound to his right leg. It looked for all the world like a knife wound. I tried to stretch my imagination and tell myself that his father had not plunged a knife into him but how could I offer mitigation for a madman.

'Marsha I don't like this at all,' Maeve moaned, 'will you please think again?

'No it's no good. Look, the "A" team'll be here soon to shuttle Mike to the hospital. See, here's the helicopter. Go on you two. Go now!' I shouted. 'Get back to me as soon as you can. Book Mike in at the hospital, then get straight back here.'

That worked! It brought us all back to the realism of the situation. I finally bid them goodbye.

'Come on Jenks,' I motioned to my faithful beast, 'let's go back down the cliff boy.'

Mike being so conveniently laid out there for us to find him, at least told me that Prescotte was here. I wondered if he could possibly have brought Bill with him. He wasn't forced to have done. Although the thought had crossed my mind, I didn't think he'd been so stupid as to have him within eyeshot. I closed my eyes trying not to think the worst. Bill could be injured, unconscious - dead! I shuddered and pulled my coat collar up further round my neck. The wind had developed a cruel, strong, cold gust down on the waterfront. Bigger waves were crashing their foam onto shiny rocks. The picture looked scarier than ever now.

'I'll tell you what Jenks.' I said aloud, fondling his lovely broad head, 'I'll bet he's holed up somewhere, watching us, now. Dear God, what if I'm right? - I'll bet I'm dead right! He's playing games with us.'

We kind of lumbered towards the first set of cave entrances making a great effort to walk slowly but the elements nearly set us into a gallop. A huge spray of water saw us jump swiftly into the first cave. That's when we came face to face with Bill's trussed up body!

My first instinct was to run to him. My second instinct was to pull Jenks back out of the cave and flick the safety catch off the revolver. I motioned to him not to move. We backed away into the open air again. Still walking backwards I heard a noise. I turned like lightening. Too late! I remember my eyes being open but saw nothing only blackness followed by a sensation of going down ...down....down! Jenks...Jenks...

CHAPTER NINETEEN

It's impossible to know how long I lay there but I opened my eyes to mostly darkness. My body shook. I knew I was shivering and not trembling. The temperature must have been zero something! I had a gag on my mouth but it didn't take long to become oriented to my new surroundings. Bill lay in front of me but couldn't speak because he had a dirty kerchief stuffed in his mouth. He looked uncomfortable to the extreme. He lay on his stomach with his hands tied behind his back and his legs pulled up and the rope looped around the bonds of his hands. I turned my head slowly in an effort to spy my dog. He must have been taken by surprise too, but where was he? So, our friend Mr Prescotte, whom we had presumed innocent for so long, was not showing any inclination of being the good guy. Had he been too fast for Jenks? Was Jenks ...

This problem gripped me far worse that the whereabouts of Prescotte. Although the greater, more immediate problem had to be, where the hell was this man. I quickly summed up my situation. My arms were bound but my legs were free. I glanced back at Bill. I hardly dare think or breathe. I had a most hideous thought that if I turned round I would see Prescotte's face. Either that or he may do something nasty to Bill and I couldn't help him or prevent it. I dared to venture a look around my new environment. It was difficult to distinguish anything in the dark. My eyes worked with diligence to establish my location. What's more, I needed to get this gag out of my mouth. There were jagged slippery edges of rock not too far from me - if I could only get to them I could edge this gag off my mouth... footsteps! Oh God this is it!

He's back. He has a gun. Must have a knife! Everything must be pristine! Now for the first time, my body crumbled into a frenzied heap. Beads of sweat pushed their way through my fringe. I could hear my heart throbbing over my heavy breathing. How long is it since I experienced such a terrifying dilemma? In fact, this could simply be my time to die! Only – it didn't actually feel that right. The time for me to die was not now! The steps came more slowly. Crunching over pebbles. Everything in my body increased in pace. Heart – thump, thump, thump! Breathing, in – out pant, pant, pant! There he was! Jenko! My Jenko bounding – bounding towards Bill and me - Jenko with Maeve and Sally in hot pursuit!

Sally ripped a Swiss knife out of her trouser pocket and tore away at my bonds. Free! God I was free! She ran to Bill. Within seconds she was hacking at his bonds, despite having to listen to Bill's sickening groaning sounds, which came in spasms. Maeve acted as sentry at the cave entrance.

Bill was in bad shape. Blood seeped through the tether of the remains of rope as Sally continued to hack away. His wrists looked like ruby rivulets. It was too obvious that the rope had been pulled so tight as to ruin his circulation and as the rope slipped away from his hands, it was as though someone had waved a wand. His wrists went from white to red to pink. They began to swell and the blood came faster. His ankles were extremely swollen. I expected a repeat performance on his ankle joints when we released them too. Jenko licked at Bill's wrists, cleaning him thoroughly.

We gently repositioned his body so that we could straighten out his tortured limbs and cushion his head on Sally's now discarded jacket. No one spoke. We had a need to work in mutual silence. Each player instinctively understood her role. Bill's whole body stiffened up like a corpse in rigor mortis. God ! Another case of hypothermia. His breathing laboured with such intensity I feared he would die there and then! Sally assured me again that an ambulance was on the way. She had actually left her mobile number too, for them to ring in case they had difficulty finding us. That jerked my memory. Where was my mobile? Where was my shoulder bag? Why in God's name was I bothered about such things now? More to the point, none of us knew where Prescotte was. He could have fled. Or he could be watching us. Sally's radio buzzed into action. We all jumped. She pressed the answer button and spoke quietly into it. Ambulance and police were not far away! God only knows how the police managed to trace us so quickly. Maybe it was because Bill happened to be an essential officer. Too good to lose! Helen's message was that they were approaching Selwick Bay, the one before Flamborough Head. They shouted emphatically down the phone for us all to stay put. They would find us. Trained-armed officers were close by now. They had warned that if we came out into the open we'd be sitting targets for our hunter. He could pick us off one by one like the proverbial sitting ducks! All panic had left me now. My only concern was for Bill. The fact that he had begun to moan and groan was a good sign.

I held his hand. 'Hi gorgeous!' I smiled down at him. 'How you doin'?'

He gasped a couple of times before he could reply. '...Thought I was doin' okay girl.'

'You are Bill! You are!' I leaned over to kiss him on the forehead but could not control my eyes as they skimmed down to his wrists. The strangeness of seeing my man crushed, so badly injured, gutted me. His wrists had swollen up badly and to the naked eye, the slight strips of fabric held fast inside his wounds as though woven together. I willed the mountain rescue helicopter and police to come faster. Come on! Come on! I slid my hand gently down his right leg. The reflex jumped. I looked back at him quickly. His smile tried to crack his pained face. I could see that the same problems afflicting his wrist, occurred in his ankles too, which in turn had hampered the whole of his circulation. In fact my poor Bill looked to be in worse trouble than when I found him recovering from a gunshot wound some months previously.

'You guys going to be alright?' Sally leaned over Bill's forlorn torso and threw an arm around my hunched up shoulder. I couldn't speak for a minute until Sally said

'Your hair's one hell of a mess Marsha Riordan!'

'Why thank you Sally. Yours seems to have adopted a strange stance too if I may say. It looks kind of stupid at the back, where the wind has flattened it - you know, like you have a head shaped like that Tefal advert. If you had a mirror you'd see that your face is incredibly white in this half-light too - sort of alien-like!'

That set Bill off. In fact that set us all off. No, it simply wasn't particularly funny at all. But we all laughed so loudly, in fact hysterically that we didn't hear our rescuers until they were on top of us.

The paramedics could sense immediately by our mental and physical state that we were all in shock. The laughter had been a tonic in itself. The armed police came into our cave backwards looking every which way for a possible sniper or rather a possible "Prescotte!" The medics administered oxygen to Bill before placing him on the stretcher as tenderly as they would a baby. On the way to the hospital, they began to treat his wounds to prevent them going sceptic. Because Bill had been trussed up like a wild boar, the medics thought that most of his abdominal pain could be due to strained or perhaps torn muscle.

Bill was an extraordinarily strong man mentally but I knew that it sapped his strength trying not to allow me to see his pain. Impossible! Today I knew. His eyes, the mirrors to his soul, could mask nothing. I travelled in this "flying" ambulance with my husband. Sally was bullied rather than cajoled into travelling in the second helicopter with police escort. Oh what a merry band we were. One of the medics insisted on giving Bill a sedative. As the needle sunk into his skin but before the couple of seconds it took to plunge the liquid in, Bill grabbed my jacket sleeve and grunted our loud,

'It's not me he wants dead Marsha, it's you! It's you! Tell the station! Don't stay on your...'

Of course he was telling me not to stay on my own. So - I was wrong! I thought it was Bill he was after. It wasn't, it was me! So why should he want me out of the way? I mused and puzzled while I felt every air pocket making my stomach sink and dip as we headed for home.

'How did you all get here so quickly?' I asked one of the paramedics, trying not to think so much of my own safety, at least until I knew Bill would get well and had no permanent damage.

'Well you know what a celebrity Detective Inspector Lines is Miss Riordan, your radio's were red hot girl!'

'Right!' I said wide-eyed.

Bill heard none of this. At least that was my presumption. His breathing had fallen into an easy rhythm. Thank heavens he was out of pain at last and we were on our way to the hospital.

I was quickly reunited with Sally and Maeve, reassured about Bill's health and his protection and we were then duly shipped off back home with the faithful Miguel. Astonishingly I had no visible signs of wounds, which told me that Bill must have been bound in that dreadful fashion for many hours before we reached him, from the state of his limbs.

I had tried persistently to reach into the mind of Prescotte, to try and understand why he should have done this to Bill. The only motive I could think of was sheer humiliation. If he had wanted him dead, he sure as hell would have killed him there and then. He had used Bill as additional bait to get me to a vulnerable and dangerous spot like Flamborough Head.

The police believed that he had fled and had been long gone by the time they reached us. Not me. I was not convinced. Eddie Prescotte was one smart cookie!

Insane? I didn't think so. Turned into a hate machine? Yes! What of Mike – again!

One phone call was all it took to learn that Mike had discharged himself and left no forwarding address! As if he would! Oh god! How helpful that boy *was not!* The police were as desperate to locate the boy as I was. He was supposed to be under police guard. So how had the youngster managed to fool the police guard I wonder? I then had to contact my sister to be extra vigilant. Mike may now try to reach Kerri. God only knows what for. She could do nothing.

Back over at my pad, us girls showered and sat down to a midnight supper. Hetta had wept buckets on seeing us all climb out of the various police vehicles but she had seen no Bill! On hearing of our dreadful experience, she quickly organised plenty of really brilliant high calorie-laden foods. Boy did she rant on about "plenty of sugar for shock, see" that we knew, just knew, we should not touch! However nature took its course and actually we couldn't get them down our faces fast enough. We ate fast whilst she filled a small hamper full of goodies and demanded that one of the local Bobbies take her and a hamper straight to Bill's bedside.

'Go ahead Hetta!' I'd shouted, realising that she would not rest until she had seen for herself that Bill was not on his "deathbed".

My feet were propped up on one of my huge puffy beanbags that I had hauled up next to the sofa. I loved beanbags. They filled the lounge. Sally had nestled herself into two that were opposite the sofa. Maeve had taken to an armchair and footstool for maximum comfort, whereas I noticed that Jenko had nestled into an armchair, allowing his large head to droop over the edge of it. The only person not "chilled out" would have to be Miguel. He insisted on being a waiter to us while Hetta was out. Now that I was home, I felt myself coming back to life. The brandy coursed hotly through my veins, giving me back my feeling of aliveness.

We all drank brandy. In fact I was about to ask Muiguel to fill my glass for me when he appeared and fell into the act of doing so.

'We must be telepathic Muiguel.'

'Hardly Miss Riordan – I saw your eyes look lovingly on the bottle!'

Yes that seemed reasonable. We ate and drank in real comradeship. Miguel never took his eyes off the doors. I began to think in earnest, allowing my toes to rub above and down the groove I had made in the beanbag. I hadn't tasted nicotine for forty-eight hours and wondered at myself. I could honestly say that I didn't actually fancy one now either. Survival beats nicotine every time. How could I make my resolve last? I would eat more, that's for sure, so I would have to exercise more. Oh well, couldn't worry too much. It was good to be alive! Very good!

Maeve shuffled her body around in the large beige armchair that Bill and I had picked out at an auction, only four weeks ago. She smoothed her hair down with one hand whilst retaining the brandy bowl in the other. She then very prissily straightened her skirt out and tucked the offending surplus folds under her legs. Her hand reached up to attend to her collar in order that she straighten it. Of course it had never moved. Collars of the nature that Maeve wore, simply didn't dare, did they?

They were disciplined with starch and harsh words. She had prepared herself for her little speech. Sally and myself exchanged amused glances as we all realised that Maeve would come out with something pretty profound.

'I say chaps. Do you know what I think? I think that Prescotte is still at Flamborough Head! I believe in his peculiar state of mind, he's looking for a showdown with Marsha. I think he has become theatrical, a dramatist in his disturbed state. I think he is dreaming something pretty fantastic up for you my girl!'

We could not help tittering, perhaps unkindly.

'Maeve', I sighed, 'you are not telling us anything we don't already know my sweet.'

'No Marsha,' she insisted on making her point. 'I mean I think I know what his next move is going to be.'

'Okay. We are all ears. Go ahead.'

CHAPTER TWENTY

'Well I think that he thinks that you'll make sure that Bill's well taken care of, make yourself strong and go back for a head-to-head with him. Hence the treatment of Bill and Mike. He knows now that you regard him as a fruit case...'

'...And that I'll go after him?' I finished her sentence for her.

'But if you're wise you won't do that Marsha old thing. No! You simply won't pander to his game.'

'No you're right I reckon Maeve! Only I don't believe for one minute he's a "fruit case". He's bitter, angry, and exhibits double standards. I believe he is perverted but a fruit case? No. That he is not!'

Sally stretched out like a cat, kicking her slippers off in the process, before she decided to offer me her advice.

'I don't think you should do anything at the minute Marsha. I mean let him stay out there in the freezing cold. Let him get weaker and weaker before you make your move.'

'I fully intend to Sally, although it would not be wise to underestimate him. Take it from me. He certainly won't be getting weaker and weaker. He'll be lying low, eating properly and keeping warm. You mark my words. Only ... I must be extremely careful... In fact in the morning I'll ring the station and ask them to have all the calls from my office diverted to here. That way I have my finger right on the pulse! Okay my friends, here's what I'm going to do. Apart from visiting Bill at the hospital, I'm not going to leave the house.

I shall relate all this to the Super and make sure he understands that I am doing as he wishes and staying put.' Turning back to Sally, I said rather softly,

'You know Sally, it might be useful if the police keep him running by swamping the entire area of the lighthouse. What do you think? Flush him out? Starve him out?' I paused before I said, 'and why do you suppose it's me he's after?'

'Because you sussed him love. You're only a woman. You should be subservient you see and you're not. He'd get a buzz out of confronting you and eliminating you. Women aren't supposed to get smart. Look how he treated Lucy. Drove her completely to distraction! No, he can't cope with women full stop!'

I sighed heavily, running my left hand through my untidy knotted locks whilst swishing the brandy around in my other hand,

'Sorry old state of affairs this is gang.'

Maeve shuffled her stately body about, pushed her specs a little further up onto her broad nose and looked studious.

'Marsha?'

'Mm?' I replied sleepily.

'Doesn't it make you wonder what kind of policeman, Prescotte would have made with a mind like he's got?'

'Doesn't it just?'

'I suppose,' she continued, 'if he couldn't get to you or Bill, because you're so closely guarded, how do you suppose he'll work out his next move?'

200

I shot out of my chair. I had to ring the station immediately. In panic-mode I felt I had to send a swift reminder to ask for police cover down at my sisters. I gave them the address, shouted a few swear words for emphasis and was told to calm down , it was all in hand.

Sally, calm as always, stood up, walked over to me, stroked my arm and said,

'Hey, loosen up Marsha. Everything's been taken care of. I mean every, last detail covered. The Police are working on the premise that we have a psychopath out there and a psychopath who's armed. It's okay Marsha. Really it's okay. They are not stupid!'

I regained my comfortable position of sprawled out body holding a brandy bowl, my mind working at sixty to the dozen. What would Prescotte do now? What would he try next?' I rang the hospital to see how Bill was faring. He was fast asleep. I rang my sister to see how her family were coping. The house was surrounded by Police. There were crackshots staying in the house at all times. I was pacified for the moment: so far so good. Everyone that I loved was under police guard.

I tried to be peaceful within myself and allow the conversation to buzz around the room. I glanced idly from Maeve to Sally to Muigel, the faithful bodyguard. I pictured Kerri, Mike, my Bill, everyone and slowly with the help of the brandy I let the buzz of the low talk progress without my concentration. This released me into my own world, the world that is my own private kingdom.

I sipped my brandy while events rolled through my memory. I realised that if I didn't go after Prescotte myself, he would in fact do something completely mindless, like trying and probably succeeding in kidnapping someone from my family, in all likelihood, the weakest member; someone like Hetta. No! I had to somehow get away from all this protection, and go after him, find him myself. The only one who could ever know of my plan of course was Jenks! The more people who knew, the more were in danger! That's it! I would find him on my own! I would also bring him in – that is, I would march him into the police station and let Bill charge him. That would be the only way to do it – otherwise he would continue to play games and threaten to kill someone.

It's me he wants dead. God knows why. Now this was interesting. Bill said it was because I had a sharper mind than he did. I didn't believe that for a minute. Prescotte had a sharper mind than any of us. But has he wit? Has he skill? We shall see. I had a plan.

By now we had reached one thirty-five in the morning. I made a phone call from my bedroom and on my mobile. This happened to be the only place of privacy in my small world at present. I crossed my fingers and prayed to all the gods, that the recipient of the call would not mind the hour that I chose to disturb him.

'Randolph, Marsha here. Look I apologise sincerely for the lateness of the call. Could I possibly meet you over in our gym tomorrow morning at seven thirty. I shall have Miguel as bodyguard.'

The line was silent for seconds that stretched into hours in my head, before the gentle voice at the other end said,

'My dear I've been expecting your call for days and have prepared myself to be at your service for as long as you need me. How are you by the way? Not drinking alcohol I hope.'

'Well yes Randolph I am, but I will stop – I mean I will put it down - now you're laughing at me you old goat.'

'Tomorrow. Seven thirty will be fine. See you in the morning. Sleep well.'

I bid him good night and could picture him so well in my mind's eye. All lean six feet of him. Randolph was one of three teachers from whom I had learnt various defence skills together with Martial Arts. He was a sixty-six years old, traditional English gentleman, a highly skilled disciplinarian and amazing cook. His face was wonderfully craggy with lots of laughter lines around his eyes that always appeared thoughtful, grey and twinkly. He had a military bearing that he'd retained from a lifetime in the army. As a friend of dad's, he kind of stood in as a distant surrogate father and lifetime friend to Bill and myself. He understood my personality and taught me how to take care of myself. It's funny but on my many adventures it has been sometimes a matter of days, sometimes weeks when I have learnt that Randolph has happened to be in the exact locality that I was working from. I wouldn't even have to tell him about this saga, he would know every detail before I met him. Now that I had at least taken some initiative over protecting myself, I felt as though I could sleep.

I set the alarm for six o'clock so that I could make myself eat a healthy breakfast and perhaps get away with smoking a couple of cigarettes. I would receive a harsh lecture on smoking and may have to agree to acupuncture or some other such cure for my disgusting habit before I am allowed to leave his company.

Muigel, true to his word had set his alarm too. He would engage in a workout whilst I fought and trained with my guru. We took Jenks of course. I would never have got away with visiting Randolph without Jenks. They were big buddies, I mean mega-big buddies. The rapport those two have between them is uncanny so as to be worrying. We see Randolph professionally twice a year. All the other times he appears, usually when there's trouble, always to keep an eye on me and I swear it has something to do with telepathy between Randolph and this peculiar dog of mine. Anyway, the three of us appeared at the gym at the allotted time.

Marcus the owner was used to us. This was a special gym. He opened at special hours. Marcus, a retired police officer, believed that most policemen and women never trained their bodies enough. He postulated that it was too easy to sink into decadence and poison your body so that it would malfunction at the time that you desperately needed it to be superhuman. Course Randolph, in strict agreement with Marcus, formed an alliance akin to a house on fire.

So there we were, Marcus, Muigel, Randolph and myself shaking hands and bowing to our respective friends. Marcus proceeded to fill the kettle which he rapidly informed us was not for coffee.

Randolph had brought refreshing herbal tea to help me begin my detox! Oh dear, I groaned inwardly.

He meant business. Miguel immediately sprang to the far end of the gym and began his warming up exercises. I was ordered to sit on the bench for the first of many lectures I would endure this coming week.

'Marsha my dear, I am so sorry but the cigarettes have to go. You have to cleanse your whole being before I can strengthen your body and sharpen your wits. You must be rid of these appalling toxins that attack your body and make you sluggish.'

'Yes but Randolph, I don't feel sluggish!' I complained, pulling a face like a chastised schoolgirl.

'That is the way that you think now, but by the time we have finished rigorous exercises of body and mind, you will be able to tell me that you feel considerably different from your present state. You may think that you feel good and fit but you are not. Shall I prove it to you my dear?'

'Oh no Randolph. I have never ever doubted you for a moment! Whatever you think I need to do in order to carry out the task I have set myself, then I'll do it.'

'Good, that is settled then. There is one proviso. I know what you are planning. Please don't presume that I am stupid and don't know your agenda, dear. You are Maxwell Riordan's daughter. Never short of courage only know-how! On this occasion, you will only carry out your plan if I am with you every step of the way. Nor will you try to deceive me, to get me out of harm's way. Now is that properly understood?' He shouted at me making his eyes appear balloon-shaped and extra-large.

'Yes I understand! Yes, I promise faithfully I will not try to deceive you, or antagonise you in any way.'

'This is understood then. You swear this upon your father's soul?' Oh dear, now we were coming down heavy.

'You're serious about all this Randolph. I can see that,' I said, bending down to tighten the laces on my trainers.

'Too damned right I am, Marsha Riordan. You're going after him on your own aren't you? Going after Prescotte on your own so that he doesn't try to harm any of your family before he attempts to kill you.'

'Right again Randolph. Didn't take you long to figure that out did it? Do you think it wrong of me to take this action?'

'No.' he said, after contemplating, his brow approaching a frown. 'I would do the same if our positions were reserved. He wants you out of the way for reasons best known to himself. If he is prevented from confronting you, it is obvious he will go for Bill again. As you have seen for yourself, if he had wanted Bill dead, he would have killed him. No, I think his mind has a fixed turn towards misogyny. You need expert help here Marsha. I work in a different manner from the police. We need to outwit him. You must promise me now, otherwise I will "blow" your game to the Police.'

I promised!

We paced ourselves. Strenuous physical and mental exercises coupled with herbal tea. Herbal snacks and more mental exercises were the order of the day. No cigarettes or alcohol could pass my ruby lips! In fact this whole darned carry on went on for ten days. It would have gone another couple of days but we daren't run the risk of leaving Prescotte any longer.

He would by now, we thought, be living roughly in the caves at Flamborough. The police had made a "sweep" of Flambrough and it's caves yet their search had produced nothing. Prescotte had either escaped or was still well-hidden.

I thought the latter, although we all regarded him as having an almighty fine brain for us to pit our wits against, he would be running on anger not rationality. That point levelling on our side, I had also had to be conniving enough to keep Bill in hospital. I had managed this by insisting that he go into a private ward for his nursing care, to get a complete recovery and rest.

I had convinced him that he had not looked after his body properly beforehand and that now was an excellent opportunity to do so. It was not a lie. Bill did not give himself ample rest. The job would not allow him to eat his meals at the correct time. In my opinion, he worked tremendously long hours with insufficient sleep to rest up, coupled with a distinct lack of exercise. So, I had successfully talked him round to having a complete health check and rest that would take up to a fortnight. Our police officers liaised every day to check on Kerri and my sister's family.All was well so far. The only missing link that may prove to be problematic was Mike. Randolph was well aware of all the problems and felt especially for Mike, whom he decided would become his full responsibility after getting Prescotte behind bars.

CHAPTER TWENTY-ONE

Today was the day. The only person taken into our confidence as regards our plan, was Miguel. Guilt ravaged my mind but I had to put that particular problem into hiding until my task was completed. My dear friends and Bill would be horrified if they knew what I was about to attempt. Miguel and I set off as if we were going to the gym. We had bottled spring water, fresh fruit and chocolate-coated Kendal mint cake, which would serve a normal day's pack up, as though we were going for a workout. Only we weren't. We were heading for Flamborough Head. First of all we were to pick up Randolph. As a marked reward for my pains, if all went well, I could in fact hit the caffeine plus some of the indulgences I had kept away from myself. I would have to wrestle when it came to the nicotine though. I must confess I had never felt better physically or mentally after my complete bodily "clean-out" and "psyche-out".

We had radios and mobile phones for immediate communication. I also argued quite ferociously with Muiguel over what I was doing. I had to make him promise not to tell his superiors, at least not unless we were in dire straits and on point of death. Muigel would only agree if he came with us and was "in on it". So we took a leisurely drive over to the gym, after running Jenks and ringing the hospital to check that Bill was all right. We had decided that we would spend a careful period of time, searching, being as casual as possible trying to find Prescotte's hideaway, so that we did not arouse too much suspicion. The more people that became involved, the greater the risk of the loss of life became a possibility.

Randolph leaned lazily against the newly painted

gateway at the entrance to the gym looking for all the world like someone's grandad waiting for a lift on a family outing. Yet even when he supposed that he was looking laid-back, dressed down, in old-fashioned clothes, wearing spectacles with clear glass because his eyesight was perfect, even after all that, there was an air about him: something indefinable, something strong and charismatic that made him stand apart. Or was it simply me who could see all that?

I waved Randolph over, gesticulating to him to jump in. He motioned with a shake of the head that he was not coming in the car. We were to go into the gym ahead of him. Now his casual stance told us nothing. There could be trouble! He called for Jenks who obeyed immediately! We all trouped in following the bouncing, bounding animal. He didn't need any directions as to which room he was supposed to be going to. He went straight for the First Aid room.

'Hello Marsha,' sobbed the tearful voice before he collapsed in my arms sobbing as if his very heart would break. Mike could say no more. Not yet! He could hold on to me! His arms held my neck, his head in my bosom. I could not help myself, I cried with him. I cried for his mother! I cried for his pain, for his great loss. Never again would he have a normal family life. Never again would he go home from college on vacation. There was no family left. He knew that his father would either rot in prison after capture or be killed resisting.

Randolph gently prised the boy's resisting fingers from around my neck and tenderly moved his head from my chest over to his own. No one spoke. He sat down on the stretcher bed and cuddled Mike like a little baby. I realised then, that he had found Randolph some time ago. Randolph pointed to the kettle and also to the water dish on the floor that Jenko had promptly emptied. He wanted us to do ordinary things. Put the kettle on for coffee! At least I hoped I could have a real coffee.

This tense atmosphere recommended either nicotine or caffeine to help it over its climax. Randolph would not allow me to smoke on his premises anyway, no matter how difficult a time we were having. I could get nothing out of Mike only "sorry". If he said it once, he said it fifty times. He was young and imagined himself completely alone in the world now. Randolph cradled him in his arms for some time.

Muigel and I walked through to the apparatus and left them alone. It was some forty-five minutes later that Randolph strode confidently back to us and suggested we got on with the job in hand. Both Muigel and I jumped in with a million questions all with reference to Mike. Nothing was forthcoming as he waved a hand and shrugged as if to say, "not now. It is inappropriate".

Randolph then had us bundle ourselves sharply into the car explaining very little. What he did say was that Mike would remain with him indefinitely and would be kept quite safe whilst we tried to find his father and bring him to justice. In other words, as much as he loved and cared for us, Randolph had taken Mike under his wing and it was not for us to know how he would help him back to a normal life. It was enough to know that I was totally confident that he would do it most successfully.

On we sped now in the trusty Volvo. We chatted in great camaraderie. Although Randolph had a new adopted child he never neglected the ones he had adopted previously, like our gang. He was a strange man.

He gave off an ethereal air as though he came from another planet. Sometimes in my more fanciful moments I would tell myself he was another guardian angel that dad had sent down from wherever he was dwelling. I had come in touch with, I would think, four of these angels during my adventures and teaching years. You know the feeling; that someone is looking after you. Coincidence? Serendipity? Who knows? But it does appear to work: appear being the operative word. Someone always appears at the right time!

'Is there any particular time that you need to be home, Randolph?' I asked as easily as I could, not wanting my question to sound as though I was fishing for information – any kind of information!

'No, no dear girl. Thank you for asking. It is thoughtful of you to consider me!' he said politely, smiling cheekily as I glanced at him in my front mirror.

'That's all right then. We can go for it then, can we?' I enthused.

'Certainly we can. Is there anything else I can help you with apart from telling you exactly where Prescotte is?'

I braked the car so hard I forgot that Jenks was not strapped in. No he had not hurtled across through to the front. The clever chappie was lodged between the floor and the back seat. I did not need sixth sense to know that I would receive harsh words if not lecture from Muigel, immediately after I had taken us onto a grassy area of the road. The only words I could hear being mumbled from my peers, now, was "Thank God we're not on a motorway. What then?"

'What a psycho Riordan! For God's Sake's woman! Get out and let me drive!' Muigel shouted in a raw English/Spanish drawl. 'Come on woman, get out of the driving seat. You want us all dead?'

'Okay, okay!' I gave in resignedly, jumping out of the front and into the back. Curiously enough Randolph did not "flap". He did smile benevolently whilst noting well, my seat hopping.

'Now,' I exclaimed with an exasperated authority, 'before we continue on our journey, Randolph, please enlighten us so that we know exactly where we are going and what plan of action we will take when we arrive there.'

'Most certainly Marsha. Before our abrupt stop I was about to enlighten you. You did not have the patience to drive on and store the information that I was giving you. No, you threw yourself into an emotional spasm. You will not do that again! Understand? You don't want to have us all dead and on your conscience do you?'

I opened my mouth, about to agree with him when he interrupted me again,

'No of course you don't. You must follow instructions to the full. That way we will all stay alive and we will win the day. Heh?' He finished off with a resounding chuckle. 'Now don't worry, Muigel and I will find the way. We will all sort ourselves out when we reach our destination. Relax, stroke Jenko. He is good therapy isn't he?'

I threw a warped, smarmy smile, back at him, glanced down into the big brown eyes of my old faithful animal and promptly allowed myself to relax and doze with one eye open. I remained in this position until the car stopped, which must have been about fifty minutes later. I woke up thinking of red hair and Diane Somers. In my desperation for answers I had allowed Somers to become a real red herring in my investigations. This was a fault and one that I must never fall for again! This was all to do with my ego. I wanted to be right, wanted to solve the mystery of these murders before the police did. This was unprofessional and destructive upon my character. Therefore, I acknowledged that I had learnt something!

I stretched whilst waking Jenks up, who in turn stretched pushing his great back legs into my thigh. I looked straight out of the window and realised we were back at Flamborough Head.

'Randolph what exactly is going on? Do any of us actually know? You, for instance?'

'Marsha. Ed Prescotte is hiding in the lighthouse. Although it is under automatic control, there is a sort of keeper who comes in daily to check that things are in working order. Prescotte is obviously keeping well out of sight.'

'I suppose Mike told you where he was?' My voice was softened and resigned.

'Yes. That child, for he is still a child, is at war with himself. When this is over Marsha, I will care for him.'

I looked carefully into Randolph's eyes and knew he meant every word.

'So? What now? What's the plan? I mean for a start we can't pull in any closer with this vehicle. He's going to be on the look out and let's face it, from the top of the lighthouse he's already gained a big advantage.'

'That's right,' Randolph said thoughtfully, looking out to sea, 'which is why we are going to check in at a small Bed and Breakfast and garage the car. We'll eat and get suitable clothing on for tonight.'

'We're working in the night?' I questioned, my head turned to Muigel.

'Suits me. In fact I think it has to be at night. That way it minimises the risk of hikers and bird watchers getting caught up in this mess,' Muigel answered sensibly.

'Marsha?' He too glanced in the distance to the sea, not making eye contact this time. 'You absolutely sure you want to go ahead with this? We can do it another way...' he trailed off.

'No, there isn't any other way Muigel. If we try and flush him out with armed police officers, he'd be out of here so fast you'll be looking for him a couple of hours after he's vanished. Remember, he's clever and he's not going to stop until he's outwitted and clobbered me. So when you ask do I want to be here? No! Do I need to be here? Yes! So come on, let's be organised and plan over at our lodgings.'

Muigel took the car to its allotted lock-up garage, whilst Randolph and I entered into our own personal battle, convincing the Landlady that Jenko was a Police Dog on Active Service and not a pet. It was only when I showed her my own credentials as a P.I. and produced an excellent I.D. photo with blurb to match, that I convinced her of Jenko's authenticity. It was only when Muigel waltzed in, all flashing teeth and John Wayne swagger, with his own Police I.D., that the said landlady appeared satisfied that we may actually be good guys and not baddies. Neither could she resist the yarn that she could tell no one of our presence, not even friendly gossiping to family and friends, as our lives depended upon this – a secret mission! My! How easy it is to dupe people. I knew that our lives did not depend upon her, thankfully, but Jenks was allowed in.

Our rooms were basic. We had clean beds and bedding, with an excellent view of the lighthouse from all of our windows. Luckily, our rooms were all facing the same way. We had kettles and the usual small portions of coffee, tea and tiny plastic containers of milk. I had also brought binoculars with me. Of course the first thing I did was to put the kettle on, and nip down to the landlady to ask if I could buy a proper supply of coffee, milk and sugar.

'An' 'ow long are you lot intendin' stoppin' 'ere then?' she barked.

'No more than forty-eight hours at the most. Look, this really is an important mission that we are on. Would you like me to give you the telephone number of the Chief Superintendent on this case Mrs Latchkey, so that he can verify this is all bona fida?'

'It's Mrs Latchley if I might say so and no 'course you don't 'ave to do that love. No.... I'm ...er sorry Miss. No, I'll get you the things. No extra charge either. Don't want the Police thinking I 'ain't 'elpin' 'em do I? I mean if it comes on the telly – well you know,' she said smoothing down her bleached blonde bits, hiding them under the brown bits, adjusting her pinafore as if expecting the television cameras any minute and she shot off. Within two minutes she returned with a medium sized jar of coffee, a small basin of sugar and a litre of milk, unopened. I thanked her profusely and hinted that I thought she would be rewarded for her trouble in due course.

The guys ended up in my room taking it in turns to use the binoculars while I made endless drinks for us all. Twice Randolph thought he could see a lonely figure clambering down the cliffs, but both times Miguel and I checked. It was nothing more than a couple of dogs chasing around with figures that were obviously their owners, shouting them back.

'Nice looking collie dogs aren't they?' I said to them both.

'Yes Marsha, handsome, beautiful, fantastic, only we're not that interested in collie dogs are we?' That was Muigel being funny.

'No, I don't suppose we're that interested in their owner either are we?' I beckoned them over to the window and handed them the binocs. in turn to see if they could get an angle on the dog owner.

'What are we supposed to be looking at him for, Marsha?'

'Do you have him? Can you see him?' I gasped, mocking enthusiasm.

'Yes,' they both said, as if I was some kind of a student at playschool.

'So,' I followed up quickly, 'exactly how do you know that the dog owner is not Prescotte?'

Muigel took another look.

'Easy! That guy is dressed up to the nines in hiking gear, you know the right gear for being out here.

216

Prescotte isn't.'

'How do you know that from here?' I questioned again. 'Randolph you know that we cannot dismiss anything, any possibility. Isn't that right?'

'Of course Marsha, you are quite correct. We must presume nothing. This man could well be Prescotte, though I doubt it.'

'Oh why?' I asked, looking for a genuine reason.

'Precisely because he will not flaunt himself in front of us. He knows we are here and he knows our numbers. He has less chance of survival if there are three of us each with a trained eye and a gun aimed at him rather than one. No, he will not lay himself open unnecessarily. Marsha you will rest for a few hours. Miguel will stay here with you. I will go and see if the hiker is what he appears to be.' He studied his wristwatch.

'I will be back promptly at seven o' clock. We will then purchase fish from the the shop across the road and ask our formidable landlady if we may use one of her rooms to eat in. In the meantime, why don't you Marsha, find the bathroom and enjoy one of your luxurious lavender baths? Miguel will stand guard.'

'But Randolph...'

'Do as I ask please Marsha.' He spoke to me in his authoritative fashion; the one he usually reserves for his students.

'Certainly Randolph. Whatever you say.' I replied,

without a hint of sarcasm in my voice. Randolph was a meticulous planner. He left nothing undone. I did as he asked. You learned quickly with him, only he did not suffer fools gladly. I did spoil myself with a lavender bath, despite my gloomy surroundings of a bare bathroom painted out in a dismal grey to match the grey and brown threadbare carpet. It may have made a difference had there been a lampshade in the bathroom but no, the bare bulb merely shone down coldly, emphasising the holes in the piebald carpet. I would have dozed, as is my dreadful bathroom habit, had it not been for Muigel's hammering on the door.

'It's a quarter to seven Miss Riordan – I mean Marsha.'

'Thanks Muigel. I'll get a move on.' And move on I did. Randolph was a stickler for promptness. Said it showed inner discipline. I needed him to have confidence in me otherwise he wouldn't permit me to go after Prescotte. I looked relaxed enough after my bath, or so the glimpse in the small half mirror suggested. This was not a time for self-admiration on any level. I was dressed in no time. Muigel and I presented ourselves in the small lounge at six fifty-five. Randolph returned at six fifty- eight. We marched across the road to the chip shop and ordered at precisely seven o'clock. We ate a non-eventful but hearty meal, (of fish minus batter!) completely devoid of conversation.

This was another one of Randolph's tendencies. If you were eating, then you were eating; not talking, reading, watching the T.V or any other such thing. There was a time for everything. Such was the philosophy that he had been taught as a young man and had adhered to for the rest of his life. Muigel made coffee for himself and me whilst Randolph made himself a wonderful cup of "green tea!" Yuk! Now we could speak.

'Okay Randolph, what did you discover, that the man with the two collie dogs really was just that?'

'Oh yes indeed! We were all correct in thinking that.'

'Yes.' Muigel and I said with apprehension knowing full well that there would be more.

'Well my friends. As you might suspect there is a ruse to throw you off the chase and also to part the three of us, so that Marsha will be so vulnerable as to put herself in grave danger.'

'Go on Randolph.' I had gripped the edge of the tablecloth. Realising that my emotions were kind of letting me down. I glanced at Muigel and noticed that he had grabbed the corner of the tablecloth in front of where he was sitting. I felt better already. The peaceful looking Randolph, whom I had never ever seen in a state of unrest, sipped his tea and waited patiently for us to settle down and stop fidgeting before he told us the rest of the tale.

'You see my dears, our clever Mr Prescotte, so enjoys games, he has employed two men the same size as himself, to dress in identical clothes as himself too. He has then issued them both with identical collie dogs. Now, you tell me about the mind of this man who will go to such lengths to create such great duplicity. All this, in order to defy the police, throw them off the scent and at the same time be free to threaten more lives.'

'Well now Randolph, that does surprise me! No, it has amazed me! This is so over the top, it's become an incredible game. But wait a minute. Did Mike actually tell you that his father would be there?'

'Yes he did. I believe he is here but I don't for one minute believe he is one of the hikers with the dogs, which is obviously what he does want us to believe. He has primed Mike well. But don't worry, I will guide the boy.'

'So where exactly do you think Prescotte is then?' I asked tentatively. Randolph put his hands tightly around his bowl of tea, for it was a bowl not a cup or mug as we normal Westerners have.

'Where he is at this precise moment I am not sure, but I do believe he is near and I believe his game-playing enters into clever disguise – I don't mean amateur, I mean clever, professional deception and illusion.'

I tutted and tugged at my hair so much that my elderly mentor stopped me in my tracks.

'It's no good becoming angry or frustrated my young friend. You must keep calm and self disciplined at all times. Now concentrate, focus - this is your aim. One small slip and it could cost one or all of us, our lives. We must study with caution. We must look deeply into every ordinary, normal situation and move that others make and remember that contact lenses, hairpieces, men's and women's clothes and shoes are all so easy to come by. What I'm saying is, Prescotte could be absolutely anyone. Anyone that is, that we do not know well and intimately.'

'Oh Lor! So where do we start Randolph? What do we do?'

'Well, we do not go out towards the cliffs at night for whatever reason. Is that clear?'

Muigel and I nodded.

'So what are we going to do?' I persisted.

'I suggest that we stay indoors this evening and rise early in the morning. For myself I'll read. I suggest that you two do the same, play cards or watch the television. We rise at six-o-clock in the morning and will breakfast at six fifteen. I will say good evening to you both. I must away and meditate a while.'

'Oh right!' I said, perhaps a little too flippantly, 'and thank you Randolph.' I watched him stand in readiness to go to his room. His bearing was upright; so powerful. In some ways, he reminded me of dad. I shook the thought away.

'What say you Muigel? What shall we do?' Engrossed in his newspaper, he didn't answer immediately.

You might wonder what Jenks had been doing all this time. Precisely nothing. The one saving grace about the bedroom happened to be a huge thick black rug. For some reason best known to himself, Jenko had adopted it as his own. He had shown no inclination to go out and leave it even for a moment. In fact, I was beginning to think that old Randolph had perhaps slipped Jenks a potion to keep him quiet. Of course I knew better. Jenks was being Jenks. Miguel thought it hilarious. Whatever we decided to do that evening, both Muigel and I had realised that Jenko would have to be walked before we retired for bed. We also knew that we had to take seriously everything that Randolph had said.

Also that every single person we encountered outside of our group was a potential suspect in this god forsaken, naked, cold corner of England.

'Okay Muigel, how about a couple of games of cards, followed by a good walk for Jenks and then unwind in front of the T.V.? There's not a lot else that we can do tonight is there?'

'No you're right Marsha. Have you a pack of cards or shall I ask the landlady?'

'No I always carry a pack with me. Come on let's have one of those small bottles of lager and you can deal a couple of hands of Rummy. What do you say? Can you cope with that Muigel?'

It seemed an age since I'd seen him smile. It seemed an age since any of us had smiled or laughed. I missed Bill more than I could say. He would be frantic now if he knew. So would Police H.Q. But I had to take a stand. I knew in my own mind that we had made the right decision. Otherwise Prescotte would play cat and mouse as long as he could. That would mean extra protection around the clock for the whole of my family and friends. It worried me that I knew the police could not really spare the manpower. Their resources were stretched to the hilt already. Catching Prescotte would solve so many problems.

We had to be sensible. I must stay in this world until we had caught him. What a grisly mess this had turned out to be. It was all very well Randolph wanting us to get into Prescotte's mind but this was not a good thing in my opinion. It is nigh on impossible to understand a sick mind and better not to try. He must be brought in, tried, and finally locked away in a safe psychiatric unit for the good of society. I would have loved to know exactly what had sent Prescotte over the top. Our minds are such fragile things, much more complex than computers. How can we hope to unravel the workings of a normal mind let alone an abnormal one?

We did idle our time for an hour and a half. I looked at the crooked clock on the wall and it said nine-fifteen.

'C'mon Marsha - time we walked Jenks. Tell you what though. Don't let him off his lead.'

'No, you're right Miguel. We don't want him running after any sweet little collie dogs that are intended as a distraction do we? We're not that wet are we? Best check with Randolph and let him know where we are going.'

We padded along the landing to his room and knocked softly. He didn't like angry loud knocks. But perhaps I knocked too softly. There was no reply. Miguel pulled out his gun and tried the door. It opened! Oh God! The room, completely ransacked, showed no signs of our friend. How the devil did they do this without making too much noise. Granted, I was bathing, Muigel had been listening to the T.V. Muigel made a sweep of every crevice and cupboard with Jenks swift on his heels. No, Randolph had disappeared and by the looks of things, not of his own volition. Now I had to think quickly here.

'Muigel, Randolph is not a man to be trifled with. Do you suppose he's let them take the advantage so that he can be taken back to Prescotte's hideout; that's presuming it's Prescotte who has him. We must consider also, that Prescotte is not necessarily on his own.

Indeed, he's obviously acquired accomplices, compliant enough to dress in the same clothes as himself, and each accompanied by the respective number of dogs in tow. He's gone to a great deal of trouble. We have to assume that whoever these idiots are, they obviously haven't a clue who he is or what he's capable of. Now where do we go from here? If we ring the police Muigel, then we might risk Randolph getting killed.' I said, praying he would have at least one constructive plan in his head.

'I think first things first. Get Jenks back on his leash. Let's walk him. It will do us good to take a breath of fresh air. We must be vigilant and not allow ourselves to be separated.'

'Yes you're right of course. Let's see to Jenko's needs first and consider ours when we've come in. I must admit I feel uneasy about all this Muigel. There's something nasty in the air. Wow, what would I give to smoke a cigarette!'

'That won't help Marsha. You need your wits about you. I could knock back half a bottle of whisky at the minute but that too, would dull my senses. Come. Let's go. And be on your guard.'

We closed the front door of the B & B. I had a spare key in my pocket. I had no idea where the landlady was but I did not think it polite to enter her quarters anyway, simply to tell her that I was walking the dog. She had given me a key so that I could let Jenks in and out, as I needed to. I felt my hair lift at the sides as the wind whipped past the door. Muigel pulled up his coat collar. I threw my scarf around my neck one more time. You needed plenty of kit on at Flamborough Head. The weather here respects no one.

'Well we're going to be limited where we can actually walk Muigel. We must not at any time, be tempted to go anywhere near the rock face. We have to stay alert. Prescotte knows full well that dogs have to be walked often. He's banking on us going to wide-open spaces so that a dog this size can run. What do you think?'

'Same as you Marsha. Vigilance is the key. Keep Jenko on a tight leash. Now let's think, what in God's name, can have happened to Randolph.'

At that comment, a voice from the darkness calmly stated.

'Nothing has happened to Randolph. Oh ye of little faith!'

My head flew round so fast I'm surprised it didn't leave my body. Muigel too did a double take, pulling the gun and aiming it into the dark shadows where the voice materialised. Then he showed himself. – Randolph!

I gasped and launched my body upon him, squeezing my arms around his neck until I almost strangled him. Muigel came and hugged him around the shoulders in a more restrained, civilised manner.

'What a pair! Come. Let's get along here. Stick to this side, it's not so windy. This poor animal needs to run don't you Jenko? You have so much pent up energy.'

'Yes, yes we all know that dear Randolph but we daren't let him out of our sight and what about you? What happened to your room?' I gasped at him

'Come Marsha. Look, it is well lit all along this road. That field too can be seen. It is at the opposite end to the cliff edge. For goodness sake let the dog go and run.'

I unleashed Jenks and let him bound off.

'He is fine. We will walk the way he goes. There are streetlights. It's well lit. Come, we'll chat while we walk. You'll remember I told you both that I wished to meditate and advised you to occupy yourselves until it was time to retire. Well I relaxed my body and positioned myself appropriately on a rug. I cleared my mind and closed not two eyes but only one. This way my concentration remains sound but I maintain a visual awareness.'

At this, he pointed to his nose as if to ask us " do we savvy?" Yes of course we did, yet neither of us could concentrate on meditation. Not only that, if anyone had asked me to sleep with one eye open and one shut I'd advise them to see a doctor! This is down to expert training in a specific field. No, I'm not trained for this, nor is my super, brawny, bodyguard Miguel. Randolph continued with his tale.

'A man crept into my room and spotted me cross-legged on the floor, presuming, foolishly, that both of my eyes were closed and that I was in some kind of trance, unable to see him. Of course I could see him and was able to judge and gauge his distance from me and also what he was about to do, which was - knock me around with a baseball bat!'

'Oh my god! No! He could have killed you.'

'My dear child, no he could not have killed me because I am not for killing. I will die when the time is right and when I am an older and wiser human being, having had the time to pass on some of my wisdom to characters like yourself Marsha.'

'Oh don't be so pompous Randolph!' I said crossly. 'You could have been killed if he had caught you unawares. You know you could!'

'No no,' he wagged his finger, 'you forget my dear, no one catches me unawares – and before you say it, please refrain from saying - not yet!'

'Okay, you win Randolph! So he creeps into your room and takes a swing at you with the bat. You can see exactly what he is doing. You stop him in his tracks, and by the looks of your room you threw one another around a bit and then he escaped with you a close second behind. You then don't think his escape is too important and let him go, which is why we now see you before us. Correct?'

'Correct Marsha.'

'Did you get a look at him though?'

'Not clearly, but I can't think it would be Prescotte. He wouldn't risk coming so close with the three of us together. No, it would have been one of his latest recruits. He'll run back now and anger Prescotte because he has not been able to put any of us out of the picture or should I say the chase.'

'Is that good or is that bad for us Randolph?'

'Actually, it is good. His anger will not allow him to think in a rational way. I told you before. You must put all emotion away when dealing with someone as disturbed as this.'

'Is he psychopathic Randolph?' I asked, hoping he would confirm my own serious thoughts about Prescotte.

'He may be but I don't think so. He is extremely disturbed and his anger is geared towards you Marsha because you are a woman. Jenko come here!' Randolph shouted after our animal. Jenks heard the command. Up bobbed the large head with the enormous floppy ears that looked like kites as he raced towards us. Randolph found him a good-sized branch to play run and catch with. All this took place at around a quarter to ten on an extremely blustery evening.

'You know what I think you two?' I chuntered, holding back the hair from my eyes and trying to keep an eye on the lighthouse. 'I think he's holed up there somewhere.'

'Why do you still think that Marsha?' Muigel asked, pushing his head into the wind and looking for the light in the lighthouse.

'Gut feeling Muigel. Intuition! So! You guys can laugh. But that's how I feel.'

But no one did laugh. Randolph nodded in agreement. 'You think so too my friend?' I nudged him curiously.

'Yes I think so too Marsha. There's really nowhere else to hide to protect yourself from the elements. You obviously would have to come out for food or send in your look-alike accomplices but I reckon that's where he is. I also reckon we have to move fast and get this whole thing over with before the police get wind of where we all are. It is going to be bad enough trying to keep Muigel's job as it is.'

'Oh great Randolph!' Muigel shot back. 'Hey don't

worry about me man! I'm going to work for Marsha anyway. I don't mind low pay for starters. I think she needs a good bodyguard. Don't you? I'm sure that husband of hers will go for it too, after this little escapade.'

'Really?' I said, pruning my hair continuously, out of my face. 'Feeling very protective all of a sudden aren't we Miguel?'

'Yes really! But like Randolph says, let's get this job done and get this headcase off the streets before he can do any more damage.'

CHAPTER TWENTY-TWO

I put my best foot forward to begin an easy stride when Randolph lurched forward, stepped in front of me, took my arm and held me back.

'First,' he said solemnly, 'we must take Jenko to the car and make him lie down on the car floor. He can't come with us Marsha. If we need him, we know where he is.'

'What'. I thought I'd misheard what he said. 'But I...'

'Now think Marsha! There are three collie dogs around these three characters, including Prescotte of course. How would you feel if a trap was set for Jenko and he was trapped by, say, three killer dogs? Well?' You must think woman. Think all the time with this man! Jenko will have his part to play later. For now he must be patient and wait.'

I knew what he was saying was completely correct but my blood ran cold at the thought of what could have happened. Randolph was right and what better trap than to capture me through my beloved dog.

'So be it my old friend! Muigel?'

'Yes he's right Marsha. We can't risk any of us. That includes Jenko.'

So it was that our adventure really began. We walked slowly but boldly towards the lighthouse with the wind blowing straight at us. The scene reminded me of high noon. Here we were, three fearless good guys going after the "baddie," only by now there could possibly be three of them.

'Marsha, do you have your gun?' Randolph enquired, with a nonchalance that belied the seriousness of the question.

'Yes I do Randolph and its loaded. You Miguel?' I asked, noting his stoicism as he braced himself against the weather; his great shoulders stiffening up so that they looked like giant coat hangers.

'Yes all loaded Marsha.'

'Then let's do it,' I heard myself say. I reminded myself of someone I had seen on the telly but kept all comments to myself. I had psyched myself up finally for my confrontation with Eddie Prescotte. Bill was safe. Kerri and Mike were safe. Now Jenko was safe. I was ready now - ready for anything. We approached the door at the bottom of the lighthouse. It shouldn't be locked. We were told on our initial enquires, that it never was. Sure enough, it was open. We began the ascent, twisting and turning as the stairs directed us.

Approaching the top we saw a man, dressed like the first collie-dog-man, run across the top of the stairs. Then we saw another one run the opposite way and yet again one more running criss-cross over the landing. Oh, now this appeared to be particularly smart game! We all rolled out eyes back as if to say, "well we've seen it all now." Was this supposed to distract us? The images were made all the more unusual as the lighthouse beam seemed to flash just at the moment of the sightings.

We pressed on regardless. We had already decided not to split up whatever happened. This was too obvious a ploy, no something else must be occurring. Of course, when we actually reached the top of the lighthouse, there was not a soul on the landing.

The small office-type room, where the actual light could be reached, was empty. So where were they? We entered the room as they do in the films, looking all about us. Each of us held both hands fast upon our guns. Every time we turned a small sharp corner, up came the gun, eyes everywhere at once. You could hear a pin drop. You could not hear us breathe. That's because we had stopped breathing until we had looked into every crevice, every nook and cranny in this room.

'Muigel – lock the door quickly!' Randolph instructed. 'Marsha over to the side of the window. Keep out of sight.' I obeyed.

'All right, everyone put your safety catches back on. There's no one in this room.'

He was right. But there had been all these bodies, seemingly, floating across the landing. Where were they all? As quickly as I had thought it, I heard a stampede of feet going down the stairs. Randolph unlocked the door and shouted for us to follow him quickly. We followed one of them as we ran helter skelter down the twisting stairs. We saw one, two, three men all dressed in the same clothes scuttle out of the downstairs door.

'Come,' said our trusty leader, 'we must catch all of them even if only to eliminate them. It may be that none of these is Prescotte but we follow only one of them. We must not separate.' Muigel put his head out first but – there was a crash, a scuffling noise, a moaning. Randolph went forward but could not see Muiguel. He pushed me back inside the lighthouse doorway.

'I'm going after Muigel Marsha. Lock this door after me. Go up into the first room at the top. Wait for us there.'

'But I can't just leave you both...'

'...Go Marsha. Get back up there! Lock the door! NOW!'

I did as he asked and tried racing up two steps at a time. This task was the most difficult. The curve does not allow for this especially with so many clothes on. I amazed myself by accomplishing it in double quick time. I slammed the door shut behind me. My back clung to the door, positively hugging it. I let my breathing continue to race, to see if it would outdo the sound of my heartbeat. Doubtful! One was pounding, the other booming. Oh God, my ears. This was dreadful. Come on Marsha get real! Get your act together. I did! I consciously made myself slow down. I didn't move. I closed my eyes and started counting slowly, more slowly, until I regained control of my body. Right - I thought, here I am at the top of the lighthouse - Why?

I wondered if this must be another ploy to get me on my own. If so, it had worked admirably. At this moment, I didn't know whether Randolph and Muiguel were still alive. But I was! Even if I felt trapped. If the idea was to separate us and put me in a vulnerable position then the idea was a charmer. What of Jenko - my beautiful chocolate partner. I had to get to him. They may even want to kill Jenko to reach me. No, I had to get out of here. Trouble was, I could see one small problem. I could see only one way out: that was the way I'd come in. I must confess to experiencing terror. Despite there being an extremely cool chill to the air, my body sweated enough to soak my clothes.

Totally alone, locked in a room in a lighthouse, I would be a fool to stay. Sitting duck comes to mind! Fire escape! Yes! There must be a fire escape! Reason told me it had to be accessible from a window. I walked steadily around the outer room looking through the windows. I could see the mist coming in and all the street lamps glaring their orange light. I could in fact see well. I felt it first, the top rung of the ladder. My imagination had gripped me in an awesome way. I half believed that Prescotte was in the same room as me. Although it was physically impossible, as there was nowhere to hide in this room, I still felt he must be here.

I fought this feeling while I made the decision to have a go at descent. I hauled myself out of the window and cautiously held a good grip on the window ledge. From there on to the ladder and hey presto, away I went. Feeling like a daredevil trapeze artist I did think momentarily how good it felt to be so far off the ground. I'd make a good pilot! But I digress. I made good my progress. Half way down I heard voices and so stopped immediately, plastering myself to the wall like a splattered fly. I heard them talking. It was clear enough. It was Prescotte's voice! Well! Now I knew where he was! But what was he saying? What in God's name was he saying? Not what I thought – surely.'

The voice was gruff, direct, 'These two. Over the side. Move 'em. Fast! Get rid of them now. I'm going after her.'

'Are you indeed?' I whispered to myself peering down, craning my neck to see what was going on. Muigel and Randolph had guns to their heads. I could hardly make it out but they possibly had their hands tied to the front of their bodies. My! How did Randolph allow this to happen? He will curse himself beyond belief!

Nevertheless, all credit due to him, he would give up his gun if they were holding one to Muigel's head. Thinking was hopeless. All of this guessing and theorising would not help any of us.

I watched them move towards the cliff edge. Prescotte moved quickly towards the bottom lighthouse door. I knew that it was locked but it stood in such a pathetic dilapidated state, it would taken only moments for him to break it down. I had to fly, be superwoman. No time! I had to get down before he got to the top and discovered how I'd escaped. I also somehow had to stall our aggressors. Otherwise we were all done for. Still the orange beam danced round and round illuminating the fragments of my present nightmare... ... Down! I'd done it. Now, I didn't follow them down to the cliff edge, I raced back to the car.

At times like these I launch into silly bargaining prayers with God. You know like "if-you-do-I-will". We've all done it. So here was my prayer. Please God, let Muigel and Randolph keep their captors talking until I can think of something! Oh and also keep their heads on! That's it God and Amen! I let Jenks out of the car and let him watch me busying myself with the appropriate tools. Oh how I desperately wanted to start up that car and drive well away from there, to safety. It would have been so easy. Jenks and me in the car, safely on the way home, would have made me ecstatic. As it happened, I might as well have whistled to the wind for what good it would have done. What good would my escape have done me with Prescotte on the run stalking me forever? None at all! I grabbed a rope from the boot and hauled it over my shoulder. My gun was primed to shoot. Now I'd had enough of this ridiculous game.

I stopped the panic from breaking into my logical thoughts. Survival was all. Prescotte must have reached the top of the lighthouse by now. Any minute, he'd come hurtling down again, much angrier than before. I was running now. I'd like to say like an Olympic athlete - I wish - stopping when I could, to recharge my batteries and ordering Jenks back into a crawl with me.

We reached the thick tangled bushes so close to the menacing area that I really did not want to tresspass. chills ran perpetually up and down my spine. I stood on something. I could just see the remnants of what used to be two mobile phones. Then as I looked towards the mayhem, I watched, in absolute horror, Muigel going over the top of the cliff. I had to clasp my hand to my mouth and hold it there. I was so close yet so far away. I could only hope against hope that Muigel had landed on a ledge.

It wasn't actually too dangerous down there: it being mostly grasses and mud, but dangerously near the jagged, slippery cliffs.

I could see that a gun was pointed downwards over the cliff edge. So that was it. Shoot them and their bodies would roll down to the water's edge and be carried out with the tide. Muigel would certainly survive the roll down the steep bank. So would Randolph but neither of them were bulletproof. That reminded me; none of us had put our bullet proof-vests on. Talk about dumb or what! Never mind that! I couldn't put that right. Both gunmen had raised their guns and aimed them directly at Randolph. He must have been aware of me by now. I wondered if he'd spotted Jenks prowling low on his belly. He had the preservation of mind to be aware but not look at me. He would not give me away. The rope around my shoulder was heavy. I turned Jenko's head towards me, kissed him on the nose end and said slowly as I looked into his eyes, 'Go for the shoulders Jenks.' Then I said.'Attack!' We were upon them. I had thrown my ropes at a set of legs. Jenks had leapt and felled one that he grappled with intensely. That gave Randolph the chance to retrieve two guns even with his hands tied in front of him. I whipped the knife out of my back pocket and released his bonds just in time. Randolph grabbed one of the men whilst Jenks held the other. The outline of Prescotte's figure bounded towards us at full pelt. I pulled my gun! I aimed!

'Stop Prescotte or I'll shoot!'

'No you won't Marsha. You're not up for this. You don't possess the killer instinct. I do!'

'Don't kid yourself Eddie!'

I aimed close to his right shoe and fired. 'Still not convinced?' I yelled at him

By now, Randolph had lashed the other one down and posed casually over his "prize" fondling Jenko's ears.

Prescotte turned and ran!

'Stop Eddie! You can't go on. There's nowhere left to run to! Give yourself up!'

'Shoot then Marsha! Shoot me if you dare!' He made back for the lighthouse.

'I'm going after him Randolph.'

'No Marsha! Wait, let's summon help now!'

'No my friend. I have to sort this out, once and for all, or I'll never be free of him. Keep Jenks there with you unless I shout for him.'

'No, wait Marsha!'

I ignored the plea. With my heart racing and my body, heaving with sweat this was a task, only I must face. I knew that Randolph would be preoccupied trying to rescue Muigel.

Now it was me racing up into the lighthouse: pulling on the railings to propel myself faster, pushing, always pushing down on my weary legs. Every muscle and sinew had been put to the test tonight by challenging my body to hang suspended one minute but motionless the next. I raced and pushed my strength to its limits. I knew there would be worse to come. Here was a head - to - head. Eddie Prescotte versus Marsha Riordan.

CHAPTER TWENTY-THREE

He'd locked the door to the main room. Was he going to stay put until I found a way in? Or would he let me believe that he was in there, when all the time he was climbing out of the window the same way that I did? The game was on! As I stood ever so still outside the locked door, I heard the key turn. The door had now been unlocked! So, this was an invitation that I could not refuse to save my life-literally!

I tried the door and felt it open so that I was able to push it slowly, enough to allow me to peep in. There he was, standing by the window, looking out into the night. He turned to face me,

'Come on in Marsha. Make yourself at home.'

'Ed. are you coming back peaceably or not?' My voice trembled. My gun aimed at his heart. I took a deep breath and steadied my hand. All the fear had left me. He laid his gun on the small table next to the kettle.

'No Marsha. You won't take me alive. I'll not rot away in prison. You have to kill me. I don't think you can do that in cold blood so I'll have to goad you into it. You see Marsha I hate women - most women that is. Funny though, I don't hate you. I have enormous respect for you. We could have made it together you know Marsha. Still could! You're a real woman. Take care of yourself. But you respect yourself too.'

I didn't hold with his flattery so his empty words flew over my head.

'Ed, is it true that when Lucy begged you to let her bring her mother over here, away from destitution and poverty, you refused her point blank?'

'Correct!'

'And is it true, that even when she held a teaching post you took all the money from her so that she still had no income?'

'Yes, that's true!'

'So why did you make Lucy lead such a miserable, intolerable life? You knew why she fell victim to prostitution. In her eyes, it was the only way she could make fast money and it was fast money she needed to help her mother. Eddie, why? Why didn't you help her? She was beautiful. She was the mother of your child. You should not have killed her. The guilt and all the blame are on your shoulders.'

'Yes I know.' He was still unruffled.

'So tell me, why did you treat her so badly and finally kill her Eddie? What was in it for you?'

He was agitated. He pulled at his hair, clenched his fingers and made his hands into fists. His eyes, which were large and an amazing, hypnotic turquoise, were flitting from this and that, from me to the window, from his hands to his feet. Was he mad, insane?

'It's women in general you see Marsha.' He looked at me for a moment or two, quite intelligently, as though we might have a proper conversation.

'...They're evil you see.' He sounded so confident.

'No, I don't see Ed. You can't generalise and say that all women are evil, the same way that I can't say that all

240

men are evil. These are non-statements. What happened to you, to make you hate women or rather to make you believe that they are hateful and unclean?'

'Why should I tell you? You probably wouldn't accept it at all. I'll die soon. You'll kill me. What good is this knowledge to you then?'

'You don't have to die Eddie. You will go to prison yes, but you'll have psychiatric care to pull you through this terrible obsession you...'

'SHUT UP! What do you know? What the hell do you know about me? Eh? What do you know you clever, strong woman? Yes that's what you are Marsha Riordan, a very clever, strong woman, in body and in mind. You'd never prostitute yourself, no matter what. Well, would you?' He gripped the edge of the table. I watched his nails dig into it with such force he would surely harm himself.

'No Ed.' I still had the gun trained on him. 'No, I'm a resourceful woman. That would never happen to me. I'd scrub floors first. There are ways. But we are not all strong and we are not all resourceful. We are all individuals....'

'...SHUT UP! Will you shut up? What the hell do you know? My mother...my mother had such a long string of men, right back from the time when I could first remember, from about four years old. She didn't hide the fact from the neighbours either. Oh no! She was so bloody showy. That's why grandad disowned her. Said he no longer had a daughter. I remember all this. I remember before he died, he warned me never to marry a stunningly beautiful woman. You'll never keep her, he said. Never keep her.

241

Beautiful women thrive on flattery, can't live without it. Need telling all the time. Need gifts. Need new perfumes, stockings, furs and hair-dos, new clothes all the time, thrills with new lovers. Granddad was right about my mother. Do you know what happened to her Marsha? Shall I tell you? SHALL I TELL YOU WHAT HAPPENED TO MY MOTHER MARSHA?' he shouted. 'She was drowned in her own bath. Years after my father had left her. Couldn't take me with him though could he. "The Social" wouldn't let him would they? Yeah, drowned in the bath by one of her lovers.

There was a big scrubbing brush lying on the bath side. They put that in a polythene bag for forensic to examine. So they told my father. Her skin was almost raw. Somebody, one of her betrayed lovers, the police said, one who thought he was the only one they said. He went berserk. Neighbours heard her screams and daren't come round. One of them rang the police. Several of the neighbours saw him running from the scene. He had tried to scrub her clean you see. Scrubbed her and scrubbed her until at last...she was pristine clean.'

His eyes lit up. He became animated, excited, smiling, 'you see don't you? Unless we men clean you up, you don't know how to be clean.' He moved forward.

'That's far enough Ed. Far enough. Listen. Just because your mother chose to have lots of sexual partners it does not mean she was unclean, or evil, or any of those things.'

'Oh, but she was beautiful. The most beautiful woman I have ever seen in my life. She had to be

242

scrubbed didn't she...?'

'.... Now hold on there a minute Ed. And what was your dad's occupation. Huh? Did he have a job? Well, did he work at all...?'

That did it. Did I ask him a stupid question or what? His laugh was loud and manic. It went on and on and on, louder and louder. Here was a really sick man. I nearly let down my guard. He sprang at me, still laughing. I jumped back instinctively.

'You're going to have to kill me Marsha,' he taunted. 'Kill me! Kill me!'

'Stop it Ed! There's no need for any of this. There was no need for you to hurt my friends either. It's you, Ed. You can't go around killing people. You have to be locked away and treated...'

I couldn't finish my sentence, he'd made a grab for my gun. I threw a mug at him across the small table. That seemed to bring him back to his senses. His eyes loomed large. They weren't looking at anything in particular, more as if he was looking deep inside himself.

'You want to know what dad did for a living Marsha? Do you really want to know?'

'Yes I do Ed. Tell me. Come on, tell me!' I shouted now.

'He was as bad as she was Marsha. He was a pimp you see! He was her pimp!' He laughed some more. He laughed and laughed until he slid down the wall. His laughter was deranged and hysterical. At that moment, Muigel lunged through the door toting his gun, swiftly followed by Randolph.

243

'You bastard, you absolute bastard!' Muigel could not contain himself.

'Forget it Muigel. He can't understand you. He is mad. Come on now, sit down over there until he calms down a little.'

'Marsha?' Came the calm, soothing voice of the old guru.

I smiled lovingly. 'I am fine Randolph. But this man here is not. Have either of you any "cuffs?"'

'Yes, I have some. Randolph fished a pair of handcuffs from his back pocket.

'Here, cuff me then. Do it. Come on. Do it. Or daren't you? I'm crazy you know.' Randolph knelt down and Muigel knelt down next to him, about to snap the cuffs around his wrists. Prescotte flipped over with his hands behind his back whisking both men off their balance. I'd already lowered my gun and put it away but he was too quick for me. He had a strong arm around my neck pulling my head back and holding his gun at my throat!

'You stupid people. You think I'm going to let you take me in? Come on! You are so slow. No, this is the woman I must take with me. We will die together. She is untainted, one of a kind, the best. She will die before she can be tainted.' Muigel moved forward as if to make a grab for him.

'Get back,' he yelled and trod on Muigel's hand as he tried to retrieve one of the guns. 'Get back or I'll kill us both now. Oh don't worry, it will be an exceptionally clean death. I am unsullied and so is she.' He jabbed the gun a little further into my throat. 'Get back. We're going down the steps and don't think about setting her beloved dog upon me either. I'll shoot him too! Got it?'

He edged towards the door. God knows I was going to have to walk like a crab sideways to climb down the steps. My clothes were now so wet with sweat, I felt like I'd been for a swim fully clothed. We had all sworn previously that this man was not to be underestimated, yet we had all done that precise thing. We had underestimated him.

I would never cease to be amazed that after all Randolph's lectures, his own perception of human nature had gone completely by the wayside. I had never known anyone topple him quite so easily before. But to be fair, I don't think any of us had tackled a highly intelligent lunatic before. There were no rules to apply in this situation. There can be no rationalisation. This mind did not function as a normal mind. Its thinking was alien to ours. All that can be done with it is to take it out of society. Rather like a corrupt disc in a computer, you can get nowhere with it. It does not respond.

So now what? I half-laughed to myself as I thought "that's it Randolph. Back to the drawing board with your philosophy of mankind". I do believe I'm much closer with my love/hate theories. Unless there is a true crime of passion, people do not normally kill out of love. It is usually a mind that is warped and twisted, eaten up with hate and it will treat other humans the same. This very basic thought was running through my head which still had a strong forearm wrapped around it, as I tripped, exiting the lighthouse door. I spied Jenks and I shouted,

'Jenks stay down boy. Wait. Stay! You touch my dog Eddie and I swear to God...'

'Huh? What's He going to do eh? What's God gonna do? Intervene?' You one of those that believes in the hereafter Marsha? Just think we could be exploring "over the veil" together. How about that?' He pushed and shoved, making me walk what seemed a fair old distance, in this state, until he had me sat behind the wheel of my own car. His gun was trained on Jenko but by now Randolph had his hand around the scruff of Jenko's neck.

'Don't try to follow us. You move before ten minutes are up and this car is gonna blow with us both in it.'

Well now, I had no way of knowing that this would not occur. How did I know he hadn't strapped a bomb to the underside of my car while I was up in the lighthouse and my friends being toted off the cliff edge? I started the engine up and pulled away, thankful that my friends and my dog were alive. Curiously enough, I felt more confident about handling myself now that I was alone with Prescotte. Perhaps that was because I knew it was him or me. No slips this time Marsha. One of you will live to tell the tale, the other will not, I thought hard to myself. A million things dived through my mind as I drove. Hearing this madman saying turn left, right, straight on etc., when all the time I'm seeing images in my mind's eye.

There were images of Bill, my mother, sister, nieces, Hetta, Jenks, my job, yes my fantastic job and scrubby little office. Then dad! I thought of dad! What would he do? Certainly he wouldn't take any of this crap! Never did! I know what he'd do. If he were in the very position that I'm in now, he'd swing the car from side to side until he unnerved his captor. Then he'd swing his great powerful arm across his assailant's jaw knocking him off balance enough to stop the car and think of something else! Yes that's it! But what about the something else? Come on dad, come on dad, put a thought in my head. I'm feeling pretty stupid and vulnerable at the minute. My thoughts rambled on. I was engaged in an imaginary conversation with my imaginary ghost of a dad, busy taking over any suitable logic I might have had.

For want of something better to do and not really wishing to drive out of the range of Randolph and Muigel, I did zigzag the car. This made him angry.

'Don't push your luck girl. This is not clever. Now stop it or I'll put a bullet through you skull right now,' he shouted. I shuddered as I felt sprays of his spittle shoot into the nape of my neck. How disgustingly intimate. I continued with the zigzag until I saw his eyes looking crazier than ever. I watched him in the mirror. He took the gun. I watched it, as it was supposed to come down hard on my skull.

Had I not braked hard and quickly sunk right down into my seat, it may well have done precisely that. However, this threw his concentration, on how best to shower bullets through my head. It was long enough for me to jump out of the car and away to the only route possible; the cliff edge and a roller coaster trip down to the water's edge.

As I jumped from the car, I almost tripped myself up. One of the shoelaces in my trainers had come undone. My very life depended on me not stopping to re-fasten it.

Of all the antics I had ever performed, this had to take the biscuit. As I ran, feeling every ligament and every tendon pushing and forcing, I willed myself not to think of guns, bullets or my dead body sprawled all over the cliff top. As my arms and legs were pumping to move me as quickly as possible, I knew that so were his! Faster, and faster he came, gaining on me too. Any minute now he'd shoot – I knew it – I just knew it. I had no time to decide how I would edge down the cliff, so I knew that I would do whatever came into my head. I jumped! Over the cliff top! I screwed my body up and rolled all the way down. Stones dug into me, a piece of sharp rock jutting out had ripped my jacket. A group of larger stones scraped my cheek as I rolled past them, gathering momentum. At this rate I would probably roll straight out to sea! I had to survive and hopefully prevent Prescotte from killing himself. At last - I was down! Battered but whole.

My first instinct served me well. He had started the descent. I could run along the beach and climb in and out of the hollows and mounds. Oh God! I would not get far. He was gaining rapidly now, racing towards me now like a demented buffalo. I ran a little more until he'd gained enough to be almost on top of me and then I stopped suddenly in my tracks and bobbed down. Sure enough he caved in and fell headfirst. The gun shot out of his hand. I reached it before he grabbed my foot.

'You pathetic idiot,' he growled, like a maimed animal.

'Keep back or I'll fire Ed! I mean it!'

'You won't shoot. You're not a killer. Give me that thing.' He grabbed the gun from me, because he was right. I'm not a killer. I could not shoot this man. We wrestled to the ground, by now right at the water's edge. He fought me long and hard but I was actually fitter and stronger than he was. I felt to be embroiled in a dream world. The intermittent flashing of the lighthouse beam only served to emphasise the frenetic, yet unreal action. I regained possession of the gun and brought it down hard on the back of his head. No, that didn't stop him. He started out to sea! Half running, half walking, stumbling! I followed him.

'I can't shoot you either Marsha.' He laughed the laugh of madness. 'That's a real shit! I can't kill Marsha Riordan. But you're not taking me in.'

I had now discarded some of my heavier clothing, my three-quarter coat and a fleece jacket I had worn underneath. I swam towards him and held him. This was hopeless. He put his hands around my throat and pushed my head under. I remember that feeling well enough; the pressure around my neck cutting off my breathing; the blackness, the noise of the bubbles that I let out of my mouth far too quickly, along with the tightness grabbing my lungs. It was as if I'd been trapped in a great underwater vice. This must be how you drown!

With all the strength I could muster, I threw up my arms to release myself, sprang up for air and rammed home a good elbow into his stomach. Whilst he was busy holding his stomach, I threw a hefty punch to his jaw. This put him out! He went down again. I needed help to pull him up or he would surely die. Jenks was right beside me. I wrenched Prescotte's head up and began to drag him back to the beach.

Jenks copied and pulled his jacket collar with me. By that time, Randolph and Muigel both pounced on him together and handcuffed his hands. He choked badly but Randolph sorted that out. There would be no escape for him now. None of us had a mobile phone so Muiguel ran to the B & B to alert the police and inform them that we had actually captured Prescotte and his cronies. We were safe and had done a bloody good job.

I sat, covered in two car blankets, on a rock in the blackness of the night half-freezing with my Jenks. He wagged and licked so much you'd think he hadn't seen me for years. I didn't mind the cold of the wind and the spray of the sea while I waited for the police to come. But when they did - who jumped out of the car first and galloped over to me like a thoroughbred racehorse?

'My god! My God! The minute, the very instant, I let you out of my sight what do you do? Try to get yourself killed - don't tell the police where you are - come out here with a body guard, not with police permission I might add, and a spiritual guru. Marsha Riordan you are...'

I had let Bill ramble on whilst I assumed a casual stance now with Jenko's two front paws up at my thigh. My clothes and hair were saturated. I shivered and trembled before my man. Not in fear I must say, but with the damnable cold. He finally shut up, pulled off his jacket and wrapped it around me. Then his arms came slowly around me until he could manage to speak again in a much softer way.

'How in God's name do you manage it Marsha? You could have been killed,' he whispered before he kissed me, longingly, possessively.

'No I couldn't Bill. Ed couldn't kill me when he had the chance. He preferred to try suicide but between us, we managed to stop him. What do you think'll happen to him? Will he get help do you suppose?'

'I suppose somewhere along the prison line, he will. But to be honest Marsha, I really don't give a damn about him. You have to promise me now that you'll never do this to me again. Come on now look me in the eye and promise,' my man pleaded.

Course I couldn't do that could I. I turned for a last look at the water, glanced up once again into the darkest splendour of the great where only the moon smiled down to show her pleasure and I whispered 'thanks.'

CHASTE MAN

Marsha takes her break on a visit to her Grandmother's in Yorkshire. Hardly in the house for ten minutes before the conversation becomes centred on the village priest. Gran believes he has sinister secrets and has in fact murdered someone. Marsha meets Sister Sophia, Gran's friend, who tells strange tales about him.

After Marsha's first introduction to the priest, her judgement at face value is negative. Although the priest is incredibly handsome, almost of a film star quality, his lecherous glances are out of place in a church and as part of his ministry.

Village gossip reaches Marsha's ears in no time. The priest is allegedly encouraging women, of all ages, to enjoy affairs with him. Natalie, a young blonde beauty, succumbs to his charms, then disappears. Gran's fears are that the priest has murdered her.

Marsha, after a friendly exchange of views with the priest, discovers that he is mentally disturbed, to the extent that he is consumed with self-love. His bizarre behaviour must be stopped. Marsha wishes to bring him before the courts to answer serious allegations of misconduct. The most unsuspecting person saves her the trouble.

Chaste Man will be on the shelves from May 2003

Or

Direct from BLW Publishing, 65 Victoria Road,
Barnetby-Le-Wold, Nth Lincs

WEDDING DECEPTION

Marsha Riordan, college lecturer unwittingly uncovers a clever deception after she takes up an invitation to the wedding of one of her former students. She would rather take her summer holiday now but decides to follow the saga through.

Staying in Angela's village home, she discovers to her horror that Angela is in fact an impostor and so is her brother. The dressmaker is murdered and an elaborate illusion of identities deceives the whole of the village including family and friends. Marsha becomes embroiled in an intrigue that almost costs her her life.

Her single status, which she values so highly, is threatened, as she falls in love with a sergeant on the case. She finds herself in France on a secret police operation led by a corrupt police officer. The last chapter exposes the distasteful blackmail plot against two remarkably gifted twins who have been so restricted in their movements by over-protective wealthy parents. Is it possible that they have fallen into a dangerous relationship?

Wedding Deception is available on the shelves.

Or

Direct from BLW Publishing, 65 Victoria Road,
Barnetby-Le-Wold, Nth Lincs